THE HUSBAND AND HEIR

1820: Major Buckleby seeks to marry his wilful eldest daughter, Charlotte, to his former captain, Mr Travis Williamson. However, she wishes to seek out a better match of her own choosing. Her younger sister, Rhea, wants to escape from Charlotte's temperamental outbursts, and is delighted when her father tells her that after the wedding they will travel to New South Wales. Travis is flattered by the proposition, but suspects there is more to it than he has been told . . .

VALERIE HOLMES

THE HUSBAND AND HEIR

Complete and Unabridged

LINFORD
Leicester

First published in Great Britain in 2016

First Linford Edition
published 2017

A catalogue record for this book is available
from the British Library.

ISBN 978–1–4448–3293–8

Published by
F. A. Thorpe (Publishing)
Anstey, Leicestershire

Set by Words & Graphics Ltd.
Anstey, Leicestershire
Printed and bound in Great Britain by
T. J. International Ltd., Padstow, Cornwall

This book is printed on acid-free paper

1

Rhea suppressed her anger as Charlotte threw her sewing across the room; it narrowly missed the fire that was burning low in the grate. 'You have the temper of a spoiled child!' Rhea picked up her sister's rejected needlepoint and placed it on the polished walnut table by the window seat.

'I am your elder sister and you should never talk to me like that. Do not forget your place, Rhea!' Charlotte stood up and strode toward the morning room's door. 'You may feel secure here, but mark my words — if I am expected to marry the bore of a man whom Father adores, in order to provide an heir, then I can assure you that you are not. He failed to produce a son, so I have to save the future of the estate; and once Father has gone, your future will depend upon my goodwill.' She stood, challenging Rhea.

'When he has gone where?' Rhea was bemused, as her father had not disclosed any plans to leave.

'Dead!' Charlotte snapped the word out. 'As in, gone forever!'

'How can you talk so?' The muscles of Rhea's stomach clenched on hearing her sister's passionate words. She could have shouted at and scolded her sibling, but that was what the young woman opposite her wanted. Then Charlotte would feign tears and seek out their father in the hope that he would console her as she twisted her words to place the blame on Rhea for her distress. Rhea would have felt the need to run around doing all she could to make amends and restore peace to the family.

So instead of responding with anger as she would have liked, Rhea deliberately kept her voice calm. 'Father would be appalled if he knew how coarse and cruel you can be,' she said. 'We are not royalty. This is not the home of an aristocratic family. Yes, we are landed gentry and have a working farm; yet, sister, you talk as if you are a precious princess. You should stand back a step, dear Charlotte, and see yourself in the looking-glass with clear eyes and reflect upon who you really are in the world. And please do not speak of Father's death so casually. It is beneath you … and I would never tempt fate so.'

'You can place your future in fate if you must,' her sister replied, 'but beauty can build bridges to a more lavish lifestyle. Mother knew it, and she believed in me. If only I had the chance to marry so well.' She gazed out of the tall window as if, in her momentary trance, her gallant prince would appear on his steed to whisk her away. 'If Father had only provided me with an opportunity to be seen out in society, then I would be the talk of Paris, with a worthy man at my side.' She twirled around, the white muslin of her gown billowing out. 'Am I not pretty? Do I not catch the eye of everyone when I enter a gathering?'

'Surely you do not idolise Napoleon Bonaparte!' A smile crossed Rhea's face as Charlotte stopped in shock, her hands abruptly ending their graceful line in mid-air as she spun. Instead they balled into fists at her side as she glared at Rhea. Long strands of sunshine, her mother had described her sister's golden locks. Her complexion was pale, and her jade-green eyes gleamed. What a shame, Rhea thought, that those eyes did not reveal a more kindly and generous soul. But no, she was as their colour reflected — envious and ungrateful.

'You will live to regret the day you mocked me, sister,' Charlotte snapped. 'When I am married, you will be left to look after Father, for he will never let his favourite child leave his side, will he, dear Rhea?' Her lips smiled, though her eyes did not.

Rhea thought that if being her father's companion meant that she would be able to travel with him once her sister was wed, then the feeling that welled up inside her could only be described as joy. Being left as a spinster sister with Charlotte and her future husband would, to Rhea, be a sentence to an unfulfilled and wasted life

— her own loss.

'You see, I have the name of queens.' Charlotte's chin tilted upwards as she caught her reflection in the looking-glass that hung opposite the door.

'Yes, you are beautiful, and there was a Queen Charlotte — just as Rhea's namesake was the mother of gods!' their father's voice announced.

Rhea laughed, though her sister's face flushed with rage. 'Morning, Father,' she said pleasantly. 'Have you been out riding already?'

Cold air wafted in with Major Francis Buckleby as his coat flapped open, his athletic frame still strong and upright for a man of his years, though grey hair had taken over from the once-dark line around his angular face. 'Yes, my dear.' He turned to Charlotte, who was scowling and picking at the needlepoint that she had snatched up. 'Charlotte, dear, did I interrupt a discussion?' he asked as she looked up at him with soulful eyes.

'Well, Father, I was just wondering if it would be possible for me to come out properly and visit London for the season. Miss Judith Singleton from Hazelmere Manor is, and I thought as I am nearly nineteen, I really should. Or perhaps you would prefer we did it in Harrogate?' Her face showed less enthusiasm for the latter option.

Francis sucked in his cheeks before turning around with a forced smile upon his face. 'My dear Charlotte, your poor mama's death meant that you were in mourning, and it was socially awkward for you to come out before now. However, I must insist that before you enter the marriage market — that horrid place — you understand it offends me that my girls should be viewed in such a manner by the mothers and sons who seek out a wealthy bride.'

He raised his hand as Charlotte began to protest. Her cheeks reddened and her eyes began watering. 'Nay, I do not lie — it is a marketplace!' His voice rose as his feelings were aired. 'Our lot is not so bad!' Rhea looked directly at him, and as he realised his eldest daughter was preparing to have tearful outburst, he calmed his manner.

'But, surely you want to make a good match for me?' Charlotte said. 'Do not forget that it is also a place for a wealthier, better-bred husband to be found. It is your duty, Father, to seek one out who will be able to improve 'our lot'. Besides, it would not be your daughters — it would just be me. Rhea can hardly come out unless I am first wed.' Charlotte's tight lips snapped shut as if she were biting back more critical words; she dared not speak more openly.

'That is the point. You, my dear sensitive Charlotte, must be married, in that I am in total agreement. I have a suitor in mind whom I would have you meet. Then we will talk further. Once you have been introduced, we can discuss the wedding details. He will arrive on Sunday after church, and shall stay for two weeks or so. During this time you will have the opportunity to form an opinion of him, and he of you.' He smiled generously, but Charlotte did not. 'I am certain you and he will reach an accord, and all will be well. I shall write to your Aunt Mercy to come and organise the wedding frippery in its entirety, once we have settled the affair.'

'But, Father!' Charlotte almost swooned as if the frustration of her plight would overwhelm her, but Rhea knew she was made of sterner stuff, so her action of grabbing the back of the chair and looking imploringly up at her father's blank expression fooled neither of them. 'Aunt Mercy lives in Newcastle! What does she know of society and wedding arrangements?'

He waved his hand, showing his palm in an open gesture that gently but firmly told her she had said enough, and she reluctantly fell silent. She sniffed and breathed in, placing both hands on the flat of her stomach, and smoothed down her dress.

'Your dear aunt knows enough,' said Francis, 'and is very well acquainted with Newcastle society, so do not deride her so. You should not look south all the time, for if you ever saw the fine city of London you might be disappointed, as its streets are far from paved with gold and riches, my dear.' He turned his back to Charlotte and faced Rhea. 'My dear, I need you to help me in my office. Would you join me there shortly, please?'

'Yes, Father,' she said, and smiled at him as he nodded and left them alone once more.

Charlotte turned to Rhea, her scowl destroying the natural beauty that the good Lord had blessed her with.

'He means it all for our — for your own good, sister,' Rhea said in an effort to placate the simmering storm that threatened to boil over within Charlotte, whose hand was actually shaking. However, the young woman glared back at her. Rhea's words ignited a flame of anger that resulted in Charlotte grabbing and throwing her needlepoint at the door after her father.

'Damn you and damn him. I hate you both!'

'Charlotte, you are your own ...' Rhea began, but Charlotte stormed out of the room and up the stairs, heading for her bedchamber. ' … worst enemy,' Rhea finished, shaking her head in dismay. She pitied their maid, for she would be run ragged with Charlotte's petty requests until her anger subsided and she decided to be civil again. However, Rhea doubted that, with a marriage being apparently forced upon her, Charlotte's temper would improve any time soon.

* * *

Rhea entered the study and took her position as she always did on the chair by Francis's desk.

'She gets worse, doesn't she?' her crestfallen father said as he leaned back in his much-used leather chair before she had a chance to settle upon the well-worn cushion. He looked tired.

Rhea tried to smooth the rift. 'Her moods have become more fretful since she heard that she was not going to be at the balls this season, Father. She had presumed that this would be her year to come out. Charlotte dreams of balls, assemblies and mingling.'

Francis sighed and rubbed his grizzled chin. 'I cannot allow it. Charlotte is so bothersome; her arrogance would make a fool of her with her fanciful, high-handed ways. Her mother, God rest her soul, filled the girl's head with notions of grandeur. She is a beauty, but she is not a child of grace in any meaning of the word.' He looked at Rhea, and she knew he had no illusions about her sister's character. He understood her intentions too well.

Rhea did not wish to speak ill of her mother or sister, but neither had been particularly kind to her. Her darker looks were a disappointment to her mother, as they were the image of her father's colouring. Her mother had never complimented her as she had Charlotte. That was why her sister's outbursts and tantrums had worsened in the past two years — she no longer had her mother to insist that Francis pander to Charlotte's every whim, as she was a 'delicate child'.

It was Rhea who now had his ear, and, she liked to think, his respect.

'The solution is simple, Rhea,' Francis said, 'though I hate to hold you back. I will have her settled here with a man who can look after the estate and control that temper of hers, with a kind but firm manner, while we are away.'

Rhea looked at him. He could barely control the twinkle in his eye. 'Away, Father?' She felt a rush of excitement as her heart lifted, because she had always desperately wished to travel and see something of the world. Her father had done so — in battles, mainly, which she had no wish to experience — but before that he had been on a grand tour. She had so wanted to do the same, but the world had gone mad; and countries, beautiful countries, were being destroyed as men fought for them.

'Yes, my dear. I am far from ready to end my days just yet, as your sister seems to think I will, and so I would have you come with me as I begin a little venture.'

Rhea grinned. 'I am intrigued,' she

said. 'Please tell me more.'

'See — before you know the what, wherefore and why, I have your complete trust and agreement. Your sister would pay me no heed other than to seek my blessing for her grand outing and to pay her bills for her fanciful notions. No, she will not have her way. Forgive me for being so blunt, Rhea, but that little minx could be the downfall of us if I let her loose. She thinks she has her mother's guile, but she is streets behind her. Your mother, God rest her soul, could manipulate men like a baker does his dough. Charlotte has neither the wit nor the foresight. I will have her settled — and you, my dear, free of them both. You will not be trapped into servitude to her husband's charity as an unmarried spinster, nor as a nurse to a failing father!'

Rhea saw his anger rise — a rare occasion. 'I am sorry you heard all her words just now.' She was ill at ease; no father should hear his daughter speak so thoughtlessly of him. 'Father, I — '

'Do not try to defend her, Rhea. Do

not insult my intelligence or yours. Oh yes, I heard. We shall live a little, you and I, for I certainly intend to do so for a long time to come. I have known men to wish me dead, but the heart of a selfish woman is crueller than that of a man filled with the blood-lust of war!' His fist had balled as he pressed it against the desk.

'Father, who is this man who is arriving?' Rhea asked, as she wanted to see him calm again, and so changed the conversation away from the strange manner of the major at war and back to the demeanour of the father she adored.

He looked at her blankly for a moment as he released his fist and clasped his hands loosely together instead. 'Mr Travis Williamson. He is five years her senior, and a good man. He served his time as an officer under my command and was highly praised for his service in the field. So Travis is used to doing battle.' He laughed at his quip. 'An excellent match, if I do say so myself.

'So, Rhea, go to my library and read up on the new lands — New South Wales.

You and I are going to take the opportunity of a lifetime, and put the world between you and that sister of yours!' His colour had returned to normal, but there was a hardness to the look in his eyes that made Rhea shift her position uneasily.

Her jaw hung slightly open. She wanted to travel, but this was beyond her wildest dreams. She pushed down her initial reaction to the announcement that her father had hand-picked one of his soldiers to wed her sister, without any discussion or previous meetings. She wondered at — no, more than that, she wanted to challenge — the harshness of it, but thought better of it. It would be preferable to wait and see if Charlotte actually liked the man. If not, then perhaps it would be impossible for her father to make her go through with the marriage. Time would tell.

Francis laughed loudly, as if trying to break his mood and bring back his usual merriment. The hearty, lovable laugh seemed to come from the depths of his soul, and filled the room. 'Go on with you before you swallow a fly,' he said with a chuckle.

Rhea rose, knowing that if Charlotte had heard his bellow it would only incite her temper more. However, there was no further damage her sister could do to her relationship with her father. It had been broken, and no amount of fawning would erase the memory of her words in his heart, of that Rhea was sure.

She rushed over to him from her chair and hugged him quickly, before he could read her thoughts, her doubts and her underlying sadness that their family was now fractured beyond repair. It was better that the two of them leave once Charlotte was married, and that the couple then had time to settle into married life. Excitedly, Rhea headed for the library to discover more about where her future lay.

2

Travis stretched to his full six-foot height and grinned as he studied the crack in the ceiling of the inn's room, then pulled on his worn-out jockey top-boots; they had served him well during the wars, and there was something comforting about the way they fit over his trouser legs. If only he had a fine horse to ride out of London and back to his own estate, he would be a contented man.

Standing with his shirt hanging loose around his muscular thighs, he stared out of the window, ignoring the flaking paint on the wooden frame and the torn curtain hung in a half-hearted attempt at providing privacy. He grinned. From what — gulls? He peered across grimy chimneys through a smog-filled sky. 'Glorious,' he said quietly, and smiled. He could just make out a speck of blue amidst the dirt-filled clouds. 'Here's to

Major Buckleby!' he said, before taking the last swig of brandy from his small silver pocket flask. How lucky he was to have had it restored to him; like so much of his life, it had nearly been taken away. This was London, this was grime, and this had been home for a night. It definitely seemed an improvement on the dank cell where he had spent several nights, in Newgate Prison.

Then his eyes caught sight of the letter that lay atop the crooked table next to the poor excuse for a bed. He picked it up and held it to the gloomy daylight. Oh, it looked grand enough, with its fine linen paper and red seal. The sender had taste and money, and obviously liked to show it. As he leaned on the windowsill, he knew it was from a man he owed his life to, and that also meant his debt had now been called in. If only he could simply throw it in the back of the fire and watch it burn. Would that be ignoble? Would it free him from his debt?

No! Travis was a man of honour. He was just tired and in need of remembering who he was. Looking over to the empty grate, grim and grey with no hint of flame or coal within it, he smirked. Throwing this piece of paper on that particular non-existent fire would serve no purpose. He opened the fine-quality paper and reread its contents. He was wide awake now, and, pulling his braces up over his shirt, puzzled as to why he of all the officers who had served under the major had been chosen.

If it had been an order to take part in the covert assassination of an enemy of the state, or to settle an old debt, it would not have surprised him. He was no murderer, other than in the context of war; and he had seen too much of that. That was what the taking of a man's life was called in times of peace — murder; in war it was just obeying orders, and could possibly earn you a medal depending who you killed in what circumstances. Or it could put you in a man's debt if he killed to save your life; a debt that at some point in the future would have to be repaid. At least this was not a demand for killing, stealing, or taking part in any clandestine, illegal operation. But it was more than a request; it was an expectation, or command, to be obeyed.

Travis reached out his left hand and collected his coat from the nail hammered carelessly into the wall by the door, which served as a peg, as he pondered the strange request within this summons. To his surprise and amazement, he had been rescued from his plight in gaol to attend a wedding — his own. Joy should have filled his heart; it should be flattering to be considered fit for this purpose. He was to wed the daughter of a man he respected as a soldier, and liked to think of as a friend. So why did his mood match the glum sky?

He had just rediscovered freedom; been able to walk beyond those impenetrable stone walls. The stench of the place was something he had not been able to scrub off as easily as the filth. No longer a serving soldier or prisoner, he was at one with his liberty at last — free to do whatever he pleased; to begin again. But now, out of the blue, he was to marry. If a man like Major Francis Buckleby wanted to give a daughter to him as a gift of wedlock, then he knew she must be as ugly as sin, or — he pondered the alternatives — she might be with child, or simply a scatterbrain. Why else would her father pass her on to someone with nothing other than an old family name, no entitlement attached to an estate, and only a small annual sum settled on him?

Travis was a second son, and that meagre allowance was all that was left from the sale of the family home. His dear elder brother, Alois, had seen to that while Travis fought for the very land that was being sold without his knowledge. Even news of his father's death had not been sent to him until the man was buried, and the estate settled upon the elder son, who was supposed to look after it for the good of the family. It was no wonder that, with Travis's mind so full of recent grief and the knowledge of what he would find on his return to England, his anger had overwhelmed him, and he had been drawn into a fight upon returning 'home' and ended up in gaol.

He had just been pardoned for his behaviour and released, but now he was to be entrapped in a different way. He pulled on his coat, drank the last of a jug of stale ale he had left over from the previous evening, and picked up his bag. Whatever the major's reasoning was, Travis would not question it. Whatever his demands, he would meet them. Whoever the young maid was, he would keep her safe and treat her kindly.

Included in the letter was a promissory note to present at the offices of the major's solicitor in London. His instructions were specific as always. This man was meticulous. He always had a plan; had successfully taken men through battle with insurmountable odds. Travis was to arrive looking like a gentleman — which technically he was, on a specific coach that had been paid for, at his Hall on a specific day. All the arrangements had been made. There was no escape unless Travis dishonoured his debt, and that he would never do.

So marriage and clean country air it was to be for him. With a heavy heart, but stealthy feet, he made his way from the grim streets of the inn on the edge of the infamous Seven Dials to a bath house, where a cold plunge would refresh him. Then to have his shoulder-length hair cut fashionably short and restored to its natural ash-brown hue after his brief stay in Newgate.

The new man — or that was what Travis felt like by the time he had been refreshed — took a hackney coach to the offices of Blunt, Bland and Pillman, where he was greeted by a clerk. 'Mr Blunt will see you, sir,' the immaculately dressed young man informed him after he had waited for half an hour in the chequered hallway of the tall building near Gray's Inn.

As Travis entered the solicitor's office, he was greeted effusively. 'Ah, Captain Williamson — so glad to see you. Major Buckleby told me of your bravery in the field, and — '

'Yes, thank you. However, I am no longer a serving soldier, so please just call me Mr Williamson. That will do.'

Mr Blunt stood up, but his portly frame made no little difference in his height when he stepped down from the highly polished leather Gainsborough chair. He held out a welcoming hand. 'Modesty is a virtue rarely found in soldiers, sir. I admire you even more for it. Now, I have received clear instructions from Major Buckleby that you are to be given funds and letters of introduction to outfitters used by the major when he is in town. Everything is arranged, and he is anxiously awaiting your presence.'

Travis watched as the man stood on a step by a set of mahogany drawers and reached into one that was labelled 'B'. Pulling out a file tied by a piece of dark brown ribbon, he placed it carefully upon his desk before hitching himself back up onto his chair.

'I am delighted to be able to give you these papers. There are sufficient moneys to attire you from these establishments in Mayfair and Bond Street.' He then handed over the bank notes and closed the file.

'Thank you,' Travis said, trying not to look surprised by the generosity of his ex-major, and feeling even more apprehensive about the circumstances of his bride-to-be. If he was being given so much, then she was either with child or resembled a horse.

He took the notes, placing them safely in his leather wallet, then slipped the introductions into his pocket before leaving the building. His newfound wealth was securely placed in his inner pocket of his waistcoat. He would keep it close, as he had no wish to find himself poor and helpless again.

Travis pondered as he looked through the cloud cover to a glint of blue sky. He would definitely attire himself with quality clothes, as he had no wish to offer offence, and he trusted the major to be an honest man. He owed him, and he would return that debt, even if it meant placing himself on the sacrificial altar — but not like the dandies of old, and not as a wastrel. If he was to be the major's son-in-law, he would work the estate and make sure that the family were provided for, as he would have done if he could have been present to shadow his lazy brother Alois.

Several hours later, Travis enjoyed the feel of quality cloth against his skin, and his warm feet were once again protected by fine leather boots. With the money left over from the rest of his purchases that he now carried in a leather bag, he felt like a new man. Not the tired soldier who had been down on his luck, but the country gentleman who was about to become the heir to an estate. When he thought of the proposition in those terms, suddenly renewed energy and vigour drove his steps forward. He would not be hen-pecked; he would do his duty. But Travis Williamson would lead his own life.

3

Rhea avoided Charlotte as much as she could for the next few days. One morning she rose early, breakfasted, and went out wearing her walking coat, heading across the grass to the old path that led her to the oak woods. With only a book for a companion, she found a sunny spot by an ancient tree that had watched over the estate for generations and somehow made her feel protected. When her mother had died, her father was still at war, and Charlotte's moods had changed; and Rhea had found this place, where her world could be at peace. Time never really stood still, but at least here there was a sense of continuity; something stable when everything around her was in such turmoil and her heart felt like it would break. She had lost too much already.

Her father would not have approved if he understood the real reason for her love of solitude. If he'd realised she had been so scared of losing him and her home after her mother died, he would have been disappointed in her lack of trust or spirit. She had prayed that Napoleon would not win, but wars were unpredictable. She did not have her father's confidence or arrogance that they would beat Boney as right was on their side. After meeting some of the boastful officers her father had invited to their home before he left, she had fretted deeply. Still only a child then, they had seemed immature even to her young eyes, talking of the grand feats they would achieve, those their forefathers had, and of the rabble they would lead to victory. To Rhea they had seemed full of ideas, but had little experience beyond hunting, sport, and sparring with their peers.

Rhea laughed. Her father would care dearly should it rain, because she had taken his precious book and it might be caught in the wet, whereas his daughter could always dry off and be as she was before. However, Rhea had already decided that if the weather changed, her hat would shelter the book, and she would enjoy the feel of the cool rain on her hair, as the days were unusually warm.

The prospect of going so far — to Australia, to a strange land — filled her with both fear and hope for a more exciting future. She was not so unaware of the world that she did not know that many souls were taken from their homeland as punishment and sent there in chains. Crimes had to be atoned for, she supposed; though as she looked around the estate land to the old Jacobean Hall that was her home, she felt a tinge of sympathy for what those unfortunate people went through. To be cast off into the ocean with a future of servitude ahead of you, leaving your family behind, must be truly dreadful, she thought.

But Rhea was not a criminal, so why should she fear travelling with her father? She had longed to escape the confines of her beloved estate; to travel, to see more of the world than their beautiful but isolated estate. And it was all going to happen in the next year.

Rhea stared at the passing clouds that threatened to cover the clear sky. When she returned, her sister would be a settled married woman, and her husband would have stamped his mark on their home — her home. It would have been claimed; and if, God forbid, anything happened to her father, as one day it must, then Rhea would be a dependent spinster. Charlotte might even have a child by then.

The clouds above thickened, and Rhea shivered. She would use her time with her father to see if he would settle an allowance upon her, so that in the event of his death she would not be forced from her home or into a marriage of convenience.

★　★　★

Charlotte's temper had passed, and a calm, calculating state of mind had replaced her emotional one. She had waited to see her father again; despite his set ways, she was convinced she could dissuade him from this folly if only she could be with him alone. However, he had left early the next morning on business, and would not return for five days.

Rhea, meanwhile — the little sneak, Charlotte thought — had disappeared to the library, or wherever she could hide, rather than face her sister. And so it seemed as if, at least in their minds, Charlotte's isolation had begun; but she had other ideas.

Her temper initially had caused her to break two of her mother's precious vases. Well they weren't precious anymore, she thought to herself, and smiled. Looking through the long window in the library, where she had hoped to find her sister, she decided that it was time for her to take the air too. If Rhea could leave the house without permission, then as the elder sister, there was nothing and no one who was going to dictate to her what she should do.

The smile became a smirk as her plan formed. She would not remain incarcerated in the Hall; not when there was so much she could be doing, or buying, in town. She summoned her maid. The gig would be made ready, and their footman, Jenkins, would drive her into town, where she would spend some of her father's credit. He would rue the day he sought to dispose of her so easily — so cheaply. She would come out, one way or another, and he would see that the world she wanted could and would still be hers.

★   ★   ★

Rhea saw their hooded gig being brought out of the stables along with the horse. She closed her book and stood up. What was Charlotte doing now?

She made her way across the damp grass, lifting her skirt slightly, and hastened to the front of the Hall before Charlotte appeared with her mint-green and white lace parasol, her clothes carefully chosen to match her emerald spencer and hat. Seeing her sister wearing her best day dress and fine shoes, Rhea realised that she was not intending to walk far, which was a relief at least. Perhaps, she hoped, she just wanted to take the air.

'Charlotte, have we been invited somewhere?' Rhea asked, and smiled, trying to make light of her question and avoiding, she hoped, yet another confrontation.

'No, we haven't.' Charlotte walked to the door.

'Where are you going, then?' Rhea persisted, feeling the tension in the air as Charlotte stared back at her.

'Out! I intend to spend some of Father's credit in the town. If I am to receive my future husband, then I should look like the lady of this manor and not the housekeeper! Besides, I intend to have some pretty things to look at to take my mind off your dreary plain face.' She stepped outside.

Jenkins was not just the footman; although he oversaw the horses and stable lads, he was also capable of acting as a valet, when needed, and oversaw the servants as the butler. Rhea suspected that the timid Mrs Donaldson, the housekeeper, had a soft spot for him. Jenkins was one of her father's ex-soldiers who had returned with him. That meant he was trusted by the major and no doubt indebted to him in some way. Her father seemed to attract loyalty or debts, she mused.

Jenkins's height overshadowed Charlotte as he approached and offered her his gloved hand to help her step up and seat herself in the gig. With him at her side, Charlotte looked confident and happy. Rhea watched them go. Whatever folly Charlotte was about, their father could sort out upon his return. She was not going to stand and fight when she was actually happy to have the house to herself for a time. She had wanted to travel, but had always envisaged returning to the home she loved. Yet, watching Jenkins take Charlotte along the drive, she realised that she was going to lose that home to an ungrateful sister and an unknown man. She prayed that he was worthy of it, for both her and her father's sake.

4

By the time the coach arrived in the North Yorkshire town of Gorebeck, Travis had had enough of travel and its close confinement. He did not want to wait, and so had decided to travel earlier than the major had instructed. He picked up his bag and looked around for a suitable inn where he could eat, freshen up, and seek out information as to where his destination actually was. Then he could arrange his next mode of transport to get there. He didn't see the point in buying a horse, as the major had always had an excellent eye for horse flesh and was bound to have a well-stocked stable. If Buckley was prepared to allow him to marry his daughter, Travis could not see the man refusing him an animal of his own to ride.

It was as he stood there on the side of the road, momentarily hesitating before crossing over to The Hare and Rabbit, that a gig swung around the bend of the road and into the main street. Travis took one step forward before quickly leaping out of its path just in time, nearly being knocked off his feet. He stumbled back onto the pavement, narrowly avoiding falling onto the filth and fouling his new toggery.

'Dunderhead!' Travis shouted as he regained his balance.

If the driver heard, he did not respond, and indeed the smiling face of the wench sitting next to him seemed to mock his plight. The gig sped away, slowing down to cross over the narrow stone bridge by the Norman church. Once this was traversed, the couple continued at speed out of the other side of the town. They might be laughing now, as the woman hung on the arm of her driver; but if he did not take care, the vehicle could easily upturn, and then she would laugh no more as her fine gig was strewn over a muddy ditch, with her body broken or ailing.

Travis, still fuming, made for the inn.

The sooner he found his way to the major's Hall, the better. Gorebeck had not greeted him kindly, and he had never managed to shake off the superstitions drilled into him by his governess as a child. It was time to find out what his beloved was like; and although his mood had darkened as his face had been nearly ploughed into the earth, he would lift his head high and be gracious.

★　★　★

Charlotte had not laughed so much in weeks. She had seen the man stagger as they entered Gorebeck. He was well turned out, and obviously was not someone who liked to be ruffled, as she had seen those eyes glaring at her once he set himself aright. She could always tease Jenkins and dare him to drive faster than her father did. Francis might trust him, but Jenkins was a man that she confidently felt able to manoeuvre to her will. She sensed he welcomed it because it pleased her; and because she realised he liked her more than a servant should do his mistress, the man was easy to manipulate. However, a sombre thought crossed her mind: if they had hit that arrogant stranger, her father would definitely stop her from leaving the house and using the gig unless he were there.

Charlotte sniffed as they slowed down to enter the stable yard. She had wanted to head straight out of town and continue their journey, but she could not. Jenkins would take the gig and she would slip into the haberdasher's. She knew they'd had a new delivery of silks in, as Jenkins had told her. Charlotte wanted to be the first to choose her dress for the coming season. Father might think she was not going to come out, but she intended to be prepared. Mrs Delworthy would hardly question her authority, as she had been allowed to purchase gowns there before. The major knew nothing of such things and left her to guide Rhea's choice of attire when needed for a gathering. It was high time Father invested in her apparel and a coach anyway. Perhaps she could have one as a wedding present. She smiled again; the day was not yet spoilt.

Charlotte was almost lifted by Jenkins from the step of the gig to the pavement so that she might enter the shop fresh and unsullied from the road's filth. She glanced momentarily at his hardened face, as he seemed to hold her gloved hand rather firmly while his other supported her elbow. Charlotte liked him best as the footman, because he wore a smart driving coat with its shiny dual line of buttons, and the way he walked in it made its long skirt sway out slightly as he strode purposefully along. His height and frame could carry it well. With a mass of dark ginger curls cut short, and piercing eyes the depth of oceans, he was, she decided, pleasing to the eye. Sometimes, Charlotte had noticed, they appeared blue; at others they were decidedly greener. He was at least five years older than her; but as a returned soldier who had been the son of a tenant farmer on their estate, he looked older.

She had leaned into him just for a

second, relying on his strength to steady her in order to make the step cleanly. It was in that blink of an eye, when their glances locked, that she felt most peculiar inside. It was not her stomach that had taken a turn, or a faint that overcame her; nor did her head ache. But her whole being seemed momentarily shaken from the inside out, so that even her pores tingled slightly. She stepped down, making sure no one had seen their fleeting moment of unexpected intimacy. Her confidence, so much a part of her very being, deserted her. It was as if he had seen straight into her soul — or so she thought. Had he realised? Did his lip turn up slightly, as if subduing a smile? Did he mock her in some way? Animal intimacy was something Charlotte had never experienced before; and as she turned abruptly away, she was appalled when she acknowledged what it had been, because he was no more than a common servant — a footman-cum-butler — and she was the daughter of a major and heiress to an estate. No matter what stupid sensations had emerged on a momentary whim, it would never, ever happen again. She was someone and he was not.

Without looking into those mesmeric eyes again, she strode purposefully into the haberdashery and was instantly greeted by the very welcoming proprietor, Mrs Delworthy. Charlotte was shown to a chair where she could begin viewing their most recent delivery of fine fabrics. Mrs Delworthy knew Charlotte's worth and would never cross that invisible line like Jenkins had. Perhaps, Charlotte mused, she should have him removed from her service. She would think on it; but first, while she calmed her breathing and resumed her normal composure, she would choose her fabrics and patterns, and place an order — without thinking of the moment she faced Jenkins again for their return journey, when his strong arm would support her and her body would be lifted on an invisible cloud back into the gig. She had to close her eyes momentarily to try to stop her thoughts continuing to the feeling of him being so close to her as he drove along, and the thrill of excitement that had run through her body as they sped along, nearly upscattling the fool who had just arrived in Gorebeck.

'Tea, Miss Charlotte?'

The voice cut through her reverie — thankfully, thought Charlotte as she stared at the fabric. Without looking at Mrs Delworthy, she responded in the affirmative. After all, she didn't want the woman suspecting that she was having those kinds of thoughts.

5

Rhea was enjoying having the Hall to herself. It made a pleasant change not having to put up with Charlotte's moods and moans. She was going to be a reluctant bride.

Rhea had been surprised that her father was prepared to marry his eldest daughter off in such a way. She had thought on it a great deal throughout a sleepless night. Being forced into a marriage with a man — a stranger, rather than a lover of your own choosing — seemed quite cold. Rhea was relieved that she had not been in such a situation, for she had tried hard not to imagine the intimate moments and how awkward they would be if no feelings were involved, though her knowledge of such things was vague.

Then she had reflected upon Charlotte's comments about her being left to be their father's companion. She wondered if he was equally resolute that Rhea would not marry at all, despite his words to the contrary. Once she was with him, would he let her go? She had never contemplated that prospect before, for a life without a love of her own and the children she would adore would seem a very empty one to her. Having her own family appealed to her, and yet it felt too soon; she had never been anywhere further than Harrogate or York.

Looking at the vast collection of books that her father had accrued from his travels, Rhea smiled. He had seen the world, and had a natural interest in geology and fauna. He was a strange man in many ways. Having survived many battles, he had recovered from two serious injuries. Now that he had returned home, the war all but won, he must have many a tale to tell — yet he stayed very quiet on the subject. His colleagues occasionally arrived, and he seemed willing and able to help them settle back into daily peacetime existence. But offering his beautiful daughter to one of them seemed overly generous on his part, though admittedly unappealing from Charlotte's viewpoint. Yet Rhea had not commiserated with her sister, as she did not wish it to seem as if she were gloating. Instead, she kept her thoughts to herself and pondered on the trip of a lifetime to come.

Mrs Donaldson knocked on the door of the library, interrupting her contemplation.

'What is it?' Rhea asked, and smiled, as the slender figure of her housekeeper always made her want to be gentle with her. She was excellent at organising the household and maids, but as a young widow forced into service by circumstance, to Rhea she always appeared somewhat broken of spirit.

'A visitor, miss. He has a letter from your father, but has arrived early. Should I ask him to return when he is expected? The major should not be back for a few days.' She fiddled nervously with her fingers in front of Rhea as she spoke, and then suddenly, self-consciously, dropped her hands to her sides.

'Who is he, Mrs Donaldson?' Rhea asked, and watched as the woman paled slightly at her oversight.

'Sorry, miss; he is Mr Travis Williamson.' Her eyes widened as she spoke the name. Rhea knew then that the housekeeper had overheard her father's intentions, or was somehow a party to this knowledge, as the name had meaning to her.

Now it was Rhea's turn to pale slightly. The man Charlotte was to marry had arrived early, and they were totally unprepared. She looked at the clock. It was two in the afternoon. Charlotte would not return for at least another three hours if she had gone to town. Rhea stood up; it was time for someone to be decisive.

'Please show him into the day room. I will join him there.'

Rhea's initial shock, however, turned quickly to annoyance. The man was obviously very keen. Too keen! Why should he arrive so early, and without her father's presence? Well, she would receive him, but then he could be on his way until the major returned.

She looked at her reflection in the mirror. Her few wayward curls after her walk made her look slightly windswept, so she spent a few moments trying to look more presentable. She was curious as to how this old man would appear. She even wondered if he was one of the walking wounded who needed caring for, and that was why he had so willingly taken up her father's offer of a younger bride without an introduction.

She strode purposefully out of the library and across the hallway, hesitating to take one last deep breath before entering the day room.

* * *

Travis had rented a horse from the inn to make this journey. He intended to see the major first, for a private discussion regarding the man's proposal and plans, before arriving officially, when he would be introduced to the daughter.

After his brief incarceration in Newgate, breathing the fresh country air of Yorkshire was a pleasant change. He rode along the moor road and then dipped down through forest land before approaching the estate's large gates. The Hall was more impressive than he had imagined. He had envisaged a small North Yorkshire manor house built from the local stone with a farm estate around it, but this was an elegant, symmetrically built red-brick residence. Indeed, from behind its large iron gates with unicorns depicted upon them, the whole approach was quite impressive.

Perhaps, thought Travis, the major had made a jest at his expense to show him that he had been such an idiot as to fight and get thrown in gaol. That was it — it was some sort of cruel jest to teach him a lesson, now that the major no longer held rank over him. Yet Travis already owed him his life, so why should he go to such lengths and expense to remind him how to behave as a civilian? No, there must instead be something wrong with his daughter, the bride-to-be; of that he was certain.

6

Once inside, Travis was shown by a wisp of a woman to a long room that had a fine fireplace opposite the long window. He was quite lost in thought for a moment as it brought back memories of his own home, where he would run along the gallery room in the old wing chased by his father. They would spar and laugh while Alois buried himself in his books.

Travis felt his fist tighten. He should have been there to see to his father's needs. He should have seen what Alois would do, given a free hand. His brother had taken the family home, their heritage, and sold it to the highest bidder. This bloody war had taken lives and ruined them. Travis had survived, but everything he had cherished and fought for had been destroyed. He sighed. Then, as a woman's words filtered into his consciousness, he breathed in, stood straight and smiled.

Rhea had walked into the day room where Travis stood proud, in a fine riding coat and new boots. He had been caught off guard, staring at the empty grate of the large fireplace.

'Mr Williamson, you must excuse us, for we were not expecting you to arrive until Friday … '

He watched her movements as she approached. She was beautiful in a way that shone from the inside. Her smile was polite, nervous even, which made her look vulnerable. If this was Buckley's daughter, she was very presentable.

He moved his mouth to speak, but then hesitated momentarily as he took in her face. Her skin had been kissed by the sun. She was not as pale as a young lady of breeding perhaps should be, but that, along with the dark curls of her abundant hair, added to her appeal.

'My father, Major Buckleby, is not here, and will not be for a few days,' she said.

He watched her lips as she spoke and moistened them with her tongue discreetly as she finished. She was anxious, perhaps scared even. He hesitated, wrong-footed in some way by the gesture.

Rhea began to wonder if her father had picked a hesitant fool for Charlotte. He was not the man she had envisaged, being somewhat younger than she had pictured him. True, he was handsome in a way that gave him a worldly appearance; but his hesitant nature, she assumed, would make him a pliable puppet for Charlotte to play with. This was not the man her father had alluded to, surely?

'You must forgive me, Miss Buckleby. I had hardly expected our meeting to be so … irregular. I had a letter from your father, and as I had managed to finish my business in London earlier than anticipated, I decided to ride and meet him in person.'

He swallowed, and Rhea saw what she thought could be a twinge of humour in his deep brown eyes. Did he find her plain, amusing, or inconsequential? 'Very well,' she said. 'I understand that you could not know he would not be present when you arrived.' She looked around and caught sight of Mrs Donaldson hovering in the hallway, unable to decide whether to enter or not. The major had a soft spot for the woman, but she was inept at dealing with visitors, preferring to keep a keen eye on the linen closet and the pantries instead.

'I should leave you, Miss Buckleby, and return when he is at home. I apologise for arriving earlier than expected.'

Travis stepped forward to pass, but Rhea, realising she had hardly made the effort to be a gracious hostess, had also taken a step toward him. They stopped abruptly, facing each other, no more than a foot between their faces, and it was Rhea's turn to hesitate. She parted her lips as for a moment neither spoke, both staring into each other's eyes in a seemingly awkward moment.

Rhea broke the silence. This man could have some influence on her future. She had to make this first meeting go well, but her resolve was falling apart. She raised her hand slightly to gesture that he should stay still. Then she took a step back, turning slightly as she did so to address the figure in the doorway. 'Mrs Donaldson, please have a tray of refreshments brought in for our guest.'

'Yes, Miss Buckleby,' the housekeeper eagerly replied, and disappeared from view.

'Please, Mr Williamson, take a seat.' Rhea gestured to the furniture by the fireplace. She sat down on a sofa and smiled politely, tilting her chin up slightly as she had seen Charlotte do to try and project a sense of poise. 'This is perhaps a little awkward for both of us, sir. Perhaps we should at least discover a little about each other before you leave.'

'An excellent idea,' Travis said as he chose a chair opposite her. He sat and gazed at the confident, pretty maiden perched so elegantly in her ice-blue day dress — and yet there was nothing cold about her. She held herself well, and had acted quickly to turn an embarrassing situation around. She smelt of fresh air rather than powders or perfumes. And those eyes, deep like the shade of her hair, the colour of chocolate — warm, enticing, attractive. Why, then, would the major give such an appealing young woman away to him? This situation was becoming more intriguing by the moment.

'Perhaps if I may suggest we begin by being honest with each other.' He was delighted when those eyes sparkled as he spoke.

'I prefer honesty, sir. But may I ask in what regard?'

'Do you wish to ask me a question first?' he said, and smiled. He could tell by that sparkle in her eyes that she was very tempted to ask him many questions.

'Questions about what, though?' she asked rather impishly.

'Anything. And I promise I will not deny you the truth in my answer.'

'Very well,' she replied, and cupped both hands in her lap as she stared at him. 'Perhaps you could begin by sharing how you know my father?' the young woman asked.

Travis wondered if she really wanted to know why her father should have offered her up to him — without introduction, that was — if she knew the truth of her situation. 'That is easy to explain,' he began. 'I was his captain, and I served under his command for nearly five years. He is an excellent major and strategist who is not above serving alongside his men when needed. He is brave, bold, and a bit of a renegade when it comes to getting a job done and saving the day.'

He raised his eyebrows and added, 'Now, do I get to ask you one?' He liked this game, and as her back straightened she seemed to brace herself for his possible probing question. Travis was quite intuitive when it came to people, and this lady was one he would look forward to knowing well — very well. Cautiously she nodded; she was up for a little sport and honesty, hopefully. 'Do you know of your father's intentions?' he asked. He saw her smile fade slightly.

'The wedding … ' she offered, and her colour heightened slightly.

'Yes, the marriage proposal that has been made. Are you familiar with the situation, and do you approve of it?' He had to prevent himself from leaning forward, as he dearly wanted to cross the few feet between them and share her sofa. If he could sit alongside her and feel her responses, he felt sure she would lose the hesitant and anxious air that had befallen her as he posed his direct questions.

'Now, you have asked two questions — which one do you wish me to answer?' she replied.

'You choose!' Travis suspected that she was buying time while she considered what to say. There was a third question that he desperately wanted to ask her, and that was, 'Do you carry another man's child?' She was pretty, quick of wit, and seemed healthy, so the next option for a quick, even forced, marriage would be that she had been given a child. Who the father was, and whether or not it had been a willing act on her part, would matter. She did not look naïve enough about the world to have been duped by a cad; but if so, he wanted to know who the cad was. And if it had been a willing liaison, and her heart belonged to another, he wanted to know that also. If she had instead been taken by force, then he would need to know if she had recovered and could be a wife, and of course he would catch the swine if her father had not already done so. It would have to be done silently in order for her reputation and his to stand. All these possibilities filled his mind as she answered.

'It is not my place to approve or disapprove of it.' She looked directly into his eyes, as if challenging him in some way. There was sadness there, but without asking very direct questions, he would not know its root.

'You have no objection to it in principle, then?' He watched, as she clearly felt that her words needed to be guarded. Could she really be such an obedient daughter that without question she followed her father's wishes? 'Honesty, Miss Buckleby, is the only way to build a true friendship.'

'I believe it is my turn to ask you a

question, if we are to be fair, sir,' she said, changing the subject, and it was his turn to concede and nod in agreement. 'Do you have any objection to marrying a young woman you have not yet met?'

Her stare intensified, and he saw that indeed there was a challenge there. Perhaps he had rushed this conversation and should have stayed with the safety of polite topics, but this was an unexpected chance to assess his bride unencumbered by the major's protective arm. He could discover what lay behind those dark ponds and her attractive appearance. If there was a flaw, he would tease it out. Her stomach looked flat, so if she was a fallen wench and was with child, it clearly had not been many months.

'I consider it an honour,' he replied.

'Why?'

Without hesitating, he gave her the answer she sought. 'I owe the major my life, and admire and trust his judgement implicitly.'

She looked surprised by this statement; but as she had not probed to see who his family were, how well-connected he was, or what his own circumstances were, she hardly struck him as a gold-digger. Perhaps she thought him to be one. He smiled. After all, going from being locked up in gaol to having the opportunity to be the heir of an estate was quite a leap. Or was she desperate to give her bastard a respectable name?

'You are a man of honour, then.' Her words were an automatic response, and he nodded.

'I take that as a statement and not as a question. But you are correct; I try to be.' He was about to question her further when the door opened and a tray of refreshments was brought in. While the maid was with them, they discussed the Hall and the land. As soon as Mrs Donaldson, who had stood waiting by the door, closed it as she and the girl left, their conversation stopped.

'Delicious,' Travis said as he bit into a piece of freshly made parkin. Rhea, meanwhile, used her best hostess skills to pour the tea. He watched her actions, wondering how he could bring the conversation back around to the two of them, the future, and how soon he was to be her husband. It was a strange notion — not unpleasant from where he was sitting now; but he did not want to scare her, not when they had been given this precious time together, unchaperoned and enjoying an open exchange. Then inspiration struck. He would ask about her situation and see if that brought forth any confession or awkwardness. So be it.

'Miss Buckleby, have your own plans been affected by your father's announcement in any way?' He watched her place her cup down carefully before she glanced at him.

'It came as a surprise. There had been an expectation of joining in the season when it began and coming out formally. Of course that has now changed, and ... well, plans and expectations do change, don't they, especially during times as troubled as ours.'

'You have a very forward-looking way of accepting and adapting to change;

especially one that will affect you directly. I just want to reassure you that I am a very tolerant and understanding man. I have seen more than any man should in their lifetime. I know that things can happen that are beyond our control, and sometimes, unjustly, we are left with the results. You can be honest with me, Miss Buckleby. If you know of a specific reason why your father is in such haste for the marriage to go ahead, I would like to hear it from your lips first.' He put down his plate and watched her face change as she absorbed his meaning. Her eyes told him there was something, but would she share that something with him — was she that bold or trusting?

7

Charlotte left Mrs Delworthy in a very happy mood. She had placed an order that would certainly accommodate visits to at least three balls, and also a new riding coat and accessories, a day dress and ribbons, and what her father referred to as 'frippery'. Then, as she saw their gig appear and Jenkins's fine figure driving it, her good mood faltered slightly. He always looked directly at her, almost demanding she look back into his eyes. He was their servant, the son of a tenant; and yet he had become so bold with her. Charlotte realised that her devoted puppy needed some training, yet she needed his loyalty if she was to manoeuvre around her father's plans.

She smiled coyly at him and averted her eyes from the step that would place her directly next to his fine body. She felt his firm grip upon her elbow as he steadied her gloved hand on his arm. It was strong, used to hard work; and she hoped that whoever the man was her father sought to lumber her with, by some miracle he was as well turned out as this servant was in body and dress. She would seek to capture Jenkins's soul and mould him to her will if she could not shake the man off.

Charlotte looked straight ahead as he moved the vehicle forward, and the town was soon left behind her. She kept her posture as straight as she could as they traversed the road's uneven surface.

'What is your pleasure?' Jenkins asked as they picked up speed. They were approaching a straighter section of moor road; and as she breathed in the fresh air, Charlotte looked into his beautiful azure eyes — so striking and unusual, that to her surprise the first word that came to mind, but did not escape her lips, was … *You*.

★　★　★

Rhea stared at the man opposite her and was not sure she understood his meaning. Had he heard of Charlotte's tantrums? Surely not. She was a 'minx', as their father had described her so well, but she had never embarrassed the family at a gathering — yet. To break the uneasy silence, Rhea could only think of one thing to say, and that was to ask Travis to clarify his meaning.

'A reason?' Rhea repeated. 'I am not sure I understand your meaning, sir.'

'As I said, Miss Buckleby, this is an open and honest exchange, and I would ask you directly if there is a reason for the urgency of this marriage. I assure you it will still go ahead, but I would ask you to tell me the truth, as that is the only way this can be a happy union.' He looked like he wanted to grab this opportunity to lay to rest his darker suspicions.

Rhea looked at the flickering flames and realised he suspected that there was a pressing reason why Charlotte needed to marry quickly and without any fuss. Surely he did not think that Charlotte, of all people, had fallen with child! Rhea was shocked at the boldness of his questioning, yet underneath she admired his directness.

'I do not think I am being unreasonable to ask for honesty, am I?' His softly spoken words drifted into Rhea's ears as she noted the insult that such an inference gave.

'Sir! If I understand your meaning correctly, then I do not think we have anything else to say to each other before we are formally introduced when Father returns. He is the person of whom you should be asking such ... suggesting such ... You must talk with him, for I have nothing to say to you on the matter of the marriage. It is an arrangement the two of you will have to sort out.' She stood up, as he did, and once again they faced each other with only inches between them.

'I did not mean to give insult,' Travis said; 'merely to show understanding, and a willingness to fulfil my part of this bargain. I wish only to do so with my eyes wide open and not be taken as a nincompoop.' He tilted her face to his by lightly lifting her chin upwards with his index finger. 'Please do not take offence. I would know the truth of it.'

'If you refer to immoral behaviour and the fall of a good woman, then you are jumping to an erroneous conclusion, sir. Now, I have said far too much, and you presume too much of me. I will not detain you further, and will inform Father that you called, once he returns. If you leave your address, then he will contact you when it is time for you to arrive here officially. Then we can meet in more formal and acceptable circumstances.' She stepped around him and walked purposefully toward the door.

'Miss Buckleby, I do not wish us to part on poor terms.' Travis's voice was bold.

Rhea hesitated but did not look back. 'Neither do I, but this conversation has reached its natural conclusion, and part we must. Mrs Donaldson will take down your details and show you out. Good day, sir.' She blustered out of the room, leaving Travis standing by the fire.

As Rhea watched him ride back down the drive, she admired his fine figure. He had been curious, and had offered insult; but then he was about to give up his life to Charlotte for the debt owed to his major, so why should he not be? He paused at the gates and seemed to look back at the Hall. Was he assessing its worth? Who knew the mind of a man — and one who, if he were to be believed, was acting from honour? Though there could well be a motive of greed and self-betterment within it.

One thing was for certain: this union would not be one of love. Mr Williamson was far too direct. Rhea had wondered how long it would take Charlotte to fall for his looks, charm or wit; but if he insinuated such an insult to Charlotte, she would swipe his handsome face, and that would be the last chance of harmony between them.

Rhea actually felt a twinge of jealousy; for although he was older than they, he was not *old.* He held himself well, and had spoken in a direct manner that many would run from. Mr Williamson, Rhea thought, would make a fine husband. He was straightforward, and that lack of complexity appealed to her. Charlotte never played fairly or honestly, so she would describe him as a bore. She schemed to get her own way; it was part of her fun to do so.

What a waste, Rhea thought as he rode out of sight, and she turned away to look into the gloom of the library. Not long ago she was happy in there, but she had an unbearable desire to break free and feel the sun on her face again.

★　★　★

'Very well,' Charlotte said to Jenkins, 'a little faster, but not recklessly so.'

'Hold on real tight, miss.' He glanced down at her as she linked his arm. 'Not too fast,' he repeated, but winked and sped up the straight old Roman road.

Flanked on either side by the wild beauty of the moors, Charlotte laughed and held on tightly with one hand to her hat while clinging to Jenkins with her other arm. He had bent his left elbow outward so that it formed a barrier in front of her. She felt the rush of excitement course through her body. His strength made her feel protected like she had never been before. She liked his musk; it was earthy. There was something almost animal-like about him that attracted her. He did not pretend to spar or be good with a sword — well, not the type that scored points. Charlotte knew he had been at war and thought this man really understood what life and death were. She loved the way he showed her how to feel fully alive.

He was openly laughing at her, or with her, and she cared not; for here there was no one else to see what she did. If the sheep bore witness to a lady who was behaving recklessly, then it was no threat to her reputation. It was one of the few benefits of living in the back of beyond. Her mind was free of all constraints. She cared not if her hair was a mess and if the wind whipped at the edge of her skirt. Her body's heartbeat pounded to a new rhythm. She wished it would never end. However, Jenkins was her hired man, and that was a shame; for if he were her equal or better, she would fall willingly into his arms and lose herself in those lovely eyes.

★　★　★

Travis rode up the steep bank to the moor road, leaving the wooded banks behind and seeing the amazing view across the vale appear as he reached the clearing at the top. Miss Buckleby preoccupied his mind. He liked the woman. Yes, he had offended her, and it was clear that she was not with child, for she would have been a fool to deny it when he had offered to take her on anyway. But he would soon smooth her feathers once they were officially acquainted.

He put all his doubts and fears to rest, as Miss Buckleby was a personable and pretty woman with enough wit to keep an interesting conversation going. He would have liked to offer to ride with her across the estate and see how much she knew of the land, but that would have been too presumptuous — and, as she had pointed out, he had presumed enough already. Her father had been away for years, and yet the estate was a well-kept place. It was clear, therefore, that the major's daughter must have a sensible head upon her shoulders. Even if there was an overseer or groundsman, she must have some of the running.

Many a man might not appreciate that quality in a woman, but Travis liked it; and since being at war, he wanted to find a woman to love, call his own, begin a family with, and have as a lifetime companion. Could Miss Buckleby be that person, after all? He smiled as he turned his horse in the direction of Gorebeck. However, the good humour soon faded from his features as a dust cloud in the distance revealed that infernal wench and her driver in her gig. Travis could not veer off the road into the moorland bog, and so hoped they had seen him clearly as it neared.

The driver seemed to stop flirting with the dunderhead whom he was with, and regained control of the excited horses as they slowed down to a walking pace a few yards from Travis.

His horse skittered nervously, but he calmed it. 'You bloody fool!' Travis shouted as the man neared. 'You want to kill me, or the girl, or both of us?' He spat his words out, angry that yet another accident could have occurred, and spoiling what had been a very pleasant afternoon.

The man looked at him and stopped the gig. The wench straightened her hat, and Travis glared at her as she tucked wayward hairs into her ridiculous hat.

'Captain!' the driver's voice broke the momentary silence. 'My apologies. I had not meant to be so reckless. It was a stupid whim on my part. You look well, sir.'

8

Rhea busied herself with looking through her own dresses and deciding which outfits she should wear for the coming weeks. How should she react when she met Mr Williamson officially in her father's presence? She would soon be living under the same roof — hers! The thought made her feel strange. If he married Charlotte, would he be so forthright with them both? Suppressed excitement at the prospect of such a new situation presenting itself was difficult to comprehend, as she had only just met the man.

But then her spirits slumped as she remembered that his purpose for being here was to court Charlotte, not entertain herself. Why it mattered to her what he thought about her, she did not know, but it did. Rhea realised his impression of her might be quite a poor one, as he had met her today when she had been for a walk and was not at her finest. Next to Charlotte, her own efforts, she felt, paled into insignificance.

She shook off her disturbing thoughts of the betrothal by remembering where her own path was destined to take her; so instead she decided that she must prioritise making a list of things for her travels. The weight of coat needed to fend off the north-easterlies that swept over their land come autumn through to early spring would not be suitable for the climate in New South Wales. If what she had read could be believed, the climate was much warmer, and the reverse to their own in seasons. Therefore, she had much to plan for beyond the curiosity of an eager bridegroom who would seek answers from his intended's sister to questions he should never have uttered.

* * *

'If you two know each other, then perhaps one of you would be so kind as to introduce me!' Charlotte snapped out the words as she quickly straightened her hat, unlinking her arm from the servant's the moment the gig drew to a halt. Why hadn't Jenkins told her he knew who the stranger was? Fool! She should have remembered he was no more than a country bumpkin — the dangerous sort who did not know his place, and could ruin a girl's reputation. Well, he would not undermine hers.

'Certainly. My apologies, miss,' Jenkins said, his voice more humble than it usually was, though his eyes were fixed on the stranger and not her. 'This is Captain Williamson, Miss Buckleby. He is one of your father's officers whom I served under in the war.'

Charlotte stared at the man opposite. He had not offered a nod of acknowledgment, a bow, or even a smile in her direction; instead he just stared at her. She wondered if he was so taken by her beauty that he had been rendered speechless. After all, there was no one within miles who could outshine her, even if her hair was ruffled slightly by the exhilaration of the drive. Still, he should do or say something. But instead he spoke to Jenkins, while his eyes stared blankly at her. They were a deep, unfathomable brown, not attractive like Jenkins's eyes were.

Charlotte winced as she realised she had inadvertently compared the two men — as if she could have any serious interest in either. One was, apparently, a gentleman, and the other was the fool who drove the gig sitting next to her. Surely the latter must have somehow mesmerised her, for he definitely was not a gentleman; he was a servant to do her bidding and no more. She would have to take more care that no one controlled her will, father or manservant.

'Sergeant Jenkins, you should know better than to risk the young lady's safety by driving so recklessly,' said Travis. 'Not least of which, you nearly knocked me down in the town.' Yet as he spoke, he still looked at Charlotte, as if trying to read her face.

'I am a sergeant no more, sir,' Jenkins

said, and half-smiled. 'My apologies for the incident. If I'd realised it was you ... '

'Jenkins, if I'd been a woman or a child, you could have caused injury. We are not at war now, man.'

'I apologise for my recklessness. I shall take more care in future.' Jenkins nodded at the stranger, which seemed to satisfy him. Charlotte was further enraged when Jenkins seemingly took this rebuke without challenging it or defending his driving, which she believed to be excellent, as they had never had an accident.

'Nor am I a captain, so 'Mr' will do; but my comment still stands.' The captain spoke to Jenkins, but continued to stare directly at Charlotte.

'I am in a hurry, so please, if you have nothing to say, allow us to pass, and I bid you good day.' She glared back at him, annoyed that he seemed unable to make a sensible or polite comment in return. 'Jenkins,' Charlotte said, pointing along the road, 'drive!'

'You are Miss Buckleby?' the ex-captain

finally spoke.

'Yes, I am. I am glad that your hearing is unimpaired,' she said, and obviously thought his brain was so, as it turned so slowly.

He looked away, staring behind him. Jenkins glanced at her as the awkward silence returned momentarily. Travis was still facing back down the road toward the vale as he added, 'From the Hall?'

Charlotte could not fathom how someone could be so slow of wit and yet appear a gentleman. 'Yes, from Shalton Hall — the home of my father, Major Buckleby,' she said proudly. 'If you know Jenkins, then you must have heard of Major Buckleby!'

Travis looked to Jenkins, his mood apparently darkening further. 'Good day, and take care on the slope's bend; there is mud on it,' he said. Without acknowledging Charlotte further, he had the audacity to simply ride off.

'Well!' Charlotte was livid. 'Was he such a brute in the army?' she snapped out at Jenkins.

'Oh, yes, miss. In war he was a real brute.' He flicked the reins, and the vehicle moved slowly forward as it began the descent back to the vale and the Hall.

Charlotte glared at Jenkins, for his words were lightly spoken. He had smiled as he answered, as if he had made a private jest. Well, she was not about to be made the butt of any man's whim or wit. She held firm to the seat as they went down the steep descent. Then she recalled the name Williamson — where had she heard it before? She mulled it over. Not at Hazelmere Hall, not from Jenkins or town … Her father. Mr Travis Williamson! She let out a squeal as she remembered Francis's words and intentions. She was expected to marry an ignorant buffoon!

'It's all right. Just hang on, miss,' Jenkins said as he stretched out his elbow in front of her as if it would stop her falling out.

She brushed it away. 'I am far from all right!' she shouted, and clenched her hands on the seat, holding back the overwhelming need to scream and cry at the injustice of it all. Her mother had died, and now she was to be cast off to a simpleton. She would never be that man's wife — he could not even form sentences. He had no doubt been bought his commission of captain by his rich father. The very thought of marrying a wealthy buffoon was not to be borne, for he would show her up at any ball they attended. No, she would be free of him and her father's plans. As a solitary tear ran down her cheek, she glanced up and saw two beautiful eyes staring at her, Jenkins's feelings almost tangible as he spoke.

'Don't be sad, miss. The captain will not tell the major on us. He is a good man.'

She swallowed and sighed. 'Oh Jenkins, whatever do you mean?'

He patted her knee before needing both hands to take them safely around the curve the road before them. 'Fret not. I understand, miss, but we'll find a way. You'll see.'

9

Jenkins drove the gig carefully down the steep descent and around the tight bend, needing all his concentration before heading straight through the forest and onto the Hall's drive.

Charlotte watched the building carefully from the distance. She had never really studied its great chimneys or intricate brickwork. It was almost as if she were seeing it in all its might for the first time. It was no palace, but it was older and grander than Hazelmere Hall, with its pale brick and new colonnades. Was this what Williamson craved — her home? Had he petitioned her father for her hand? What had he promised to give the major that would persuade him to give up his eldest daughter?

If the man was slow in brain, then perhaps it was his father who had some hold on hers. She must speak with the major privately when he returned and see if she could find out who was forcing his hand. There simply could be no other explanation, when his eldest daughter was so beautiful and free to make an excellent match that would lift the family higher.

She straightened her back as they slowly neared. It was as if Jenkins was making the last few moments of their journey stretch out. The peaceful silence was being enjoyed by both, their thoughts completely locked on their own paths.

Charlotte decided that she would not let Rhea see how upset and confused she was over this whole sorry affair. Instead she would arrive seemingly happy to have a new wardrobe on order and looking forward to the fittings to come. That, of course, would mean more journeys to town with Jenkins, as she had no wish for Mrs Delworthy to spoil her fun by arriving at the Hall. The woman enjoyed seeing how they lived, but Charlotte needed time with Jenkins, and to think and plan.

If her head was thumping with the turn of events, and her heart breaking with the injustice of life and the cruelty of her lot within it, then she would not share either fact with her sister. Charlotte might be momentarily down in spirits, but she was not broken. She would have both love and position.

She did not look at Jenkins again until they were about to enter the Hall, and then she casually turned to watch his fine form take the gig around the side to the stables. He held himself well. He was rough and yet also gentle. He had realised that she was upset; the man had cared. Charlotte quickly entered the Hall with her head held high, knowing that he would see to his chores with a smile on his face, as he had seen her watching him. A new challenge ensued: how to make the footman turn into a gentleman of means, so that she could have what she desired and, along with it, a man who would obey her while still moving her very soul.

Rhea greeted her sister in the hallway. 'Ah, Charlotte. I hope you had a good trip,' she began, trying to make the mood lighter on her return than it had been when she had left.

'Yes, of course.' Charlotte passed her coat and hat to a maid. 'Why wouldn't I?'

'No reason at all. Charlotte ...' Rhea breathed in, as the atmosphere was still tense between them; but she continued despite the cold chill that she felt emanating from her dear sister. ' ... while you were out ... '

'Yes, yes, you most likely read five books and had a much more meaningful conversation with Mrs Donaldson.' Charlotte tilted her head to one side and looked down upon Rhea as she added, 'You are so suited to each other. She will miss you when you are gone.' Then she dismissed her sister's conversation, no longer paying her any attention, or so it seemed.

'Why do you have to be so barbed?' Rhea said in exasperation. 'Can you not have a civil conversation with me? I wanted to tell you something important.' She was frustrated with her sister because she had decided she would be honest about having met Mr Williamson.

Instead, Rhea found it impossible to have a straight conversation with her. 'You really must listen to this, Charlotte!' Her attempt to keep the vexed tone from her voice failed.

'I only state facts. If they displease you, then return to your books, and the moths that flutter into the library amongst all those dead works of dead men written on dead trees. Live a little, Rhea — get out and feel the rush of fresh air on your face; plan a life instead of existing in Father's shadow.'

Rhea stared back, wondering what had happened to her sister; for Charlotte's hair was unruly, her manner was charged with emotion, and her words seemed genuinely driven by passion. She was usually such a cold, calculating and close woman in all but temper — and that she gave free vent to when riled. Listening to her here, Rhea thought she seemed to have come back 'with the wind in her sails', as her father would say. Whatever, Rhea wondered, had Charlotte been up to, and with whom?

'Very well,' Rhea said. 'I can see you are not in a mood to converse rationally.'

'Good. At least someone today is capable of making quick and accurate observations.'

Rhea was bemused by her sister's manner. She left, taking her coat and hat from the stand in the hall. Her day had been one of strange conversations, and she would take her thoughts outside and walk through the rose garden while there was still light. Hopefully, Charlotte would have calmed down by the time dinner was served.

* * *

Travis returned to the inn a troubled man. The letter he had received said he was to marry the major's daughter. It did not say he had more than one, or that Travis would be able to choose amongst them. Yet he had met two already. Perhaps the man had more. Was it the case, then, that Buckleby simply had too many girls, and wished to wed one off cheaply to reduce the numbers?

The one with whom Travis had sat and talked interested him; the other was a wild child who had no idea how to behave. What was more, she was far too familiar with his ex-sergeant. He had thought that he could take on the burden of another man's mistake if that were the situation, but not if it was Jenkins's child. What price was Travis expected to pay in order to fulfil his debt to the major? He had to think, and think fast.

He would arrive as expected on Sunday, but he was not going to agree readily to this request. The fair maid looked like she had talons and no decorum. The idea that he could be saddled with his sergeant's lover was intolerable. If that was indeed the situation, then she was no innocent maid who had been taken advantage of. No, she was a willing — if not leading — party in the affair, of that he was certain.

Travis urged his horse onward. If what he suspected was true — that he was to be saddled with the fallen sister — then he would somehow have to find an honourable way out, or spend an un-enviable life shared in mutual loathing; for he was under no illusion that the girl would be his willing bride. Perhaps if the little minx was as selfish as he presumed she was, then she would not submit to her father's will. Travis's heart lifted slightly at the thought. Then another thought crossed his mind: if Jenkins loved her, Travis well knew that he would never stand aside and let any man marry her. Perhaps, Travis thought, he should help the lovers run away to Gretna Green. Yes — that was it, and his own future would be safe. Then he could fulfil the major's request and willingly take on her sister.

With such pleasant thoughts, he dis-mounted outside the stable yard of the inn and entered, looking forward to a long drink by the open fire as he formed a plan and decided how he should ap-proach the major.

He had not long sat by the warmth of the flickering flames in the hearth, resting on the well-worn settle, when he heard a familiar voice ask for him at the serving counter. He leaned forward and peeked around the side of the settle, and saw Jenkins standing there. He must have dropped off his burden at the Hall and rode at speed back to the inn, to catch up with Travis so quickly.

Jenkins turned as the serving woman pointed in Travis's direction. Travis raised a hand to acknowledge him and wave him over. Jenkins strode quickly over to him, and Travis knew the man was indeed concerned.

'Sir.' Jenkins looked at him as if he were about to stand to attention.

'Sit, man. We are not in the army now.' His colleague's colour was either high from the ride, or due to the fact that he was here to talk of something personal, and Travis guessed which it was. Perhaps the truth of it would be revealed before the major returned. Then it would only be a matter of bargaining a fairer deal or solution to this dilemma. The major was a good man, but he was one who was used to being obeyed. Travis suspected that this would apply to his daughters following his orders as much as his men.

'I ... I am glad to see you well, Mr Williamson,' Jenkins began rather awkwardly.

'I am as well as I was at our last meeting, not so long ago. We fought alongside each other, shared rations, rode together, and nearly died together. I think you can now call me Travis without offering offence.' Travis smiled, mainly because he realised that he had no idea what his sergeant's Christian name was. 'Thank you, I am very well if not just a little confused,' Travis added.

'Confused, sir ... Travis? Why so?' Jenkins raised an eyebrow, but Travis knew him to be too straightforward a man to feign innocence.

'My summons here. I would like to know why it was so urgent. Do you know aught of it?'

Jenkins stated his case plainly. 'I know that you are to marry a beautiful woman who is in love with another whose heart will break if you take her from him.'

Travis saw the colour deepen in

Jenkins's face and felt pity for the man. He had overpowered many an enemy, and yet Travis was now looking at one who was about to be devoured by a she-devil.

'I'll speak plainly to you, sir, because I respect you,' Jenkins continued. 'Miss Charlotte is a beautiful, lively woman who would suffocate if you dragged her around being prissy with officer folk. She likes the wind in her hair and has a free spirit. If you wed her, you would be crushing a butterfly.' He sighed, and Travis opened his mouth to speak. 'No, sir, let me finish, because I am needed at the Hall, but would say my piece. I do wish you well. You are a man whom I admire, and have served loyally ... but Miss Charlotte is not for you.'

'Sit down, Jenkins,' Travis said, and gestured to the settle opposite him.

'I have no time, sir, but we will talk again.' Jenkins paused. 'Blake, sir. My name, the one you are searching for. Call me Blake.' He left.

10

Charlotte had a meal sent up to her room that evening, so Rhea did not see her again to discuss Travis's visit. When she arose the next morning, the sun was shining. The day felt hopeful, as did her spirits.

Looking out at the estate, beautiful yet devoid of human life, Rhea felt the need to go out and explore it. The cows were happily grazing, sheep bleated in the distance, and birds flew freely amongst the well-ordered trees that lined the drive; yet she gazed upon them like a caged bird. Well, it was time for her to fly, too. She would talk to Jenkins and find out where Charlotte had gone yesterday and what she had ordered from Mrs Delworthy. Then she would look at her own outfitting needed for the journey with her father, and ask for an estimate to present to him when he returned. If Charlotte could buy a new dress, then Rhea was quite sure it would not be presumptuous of her to make enquiries about the clothes she would need for her travels.

'Mrs Donaldson, could you ask Jenkins to prepare the gig and bring it around to the front of the building? I wish to go into Gorebeck.' The woman nodded and scurried off. Rhea shook her head; she really would have to give her some instruction about poise and how to behave when visitors arrived. Every time she tried, Mrs Donaldson looked at her like a scared rabbit about to be struck down. Her position was safe here. She ran the house well, but lacked confidence in some way. If Charlotte reprimanded her, the woman looked positively ill.

Jenkins arrived with the gig in due course. Rhea admired the way his athletic frame jumped down by the side of the vehicle as he presented himself. His mood seemed as light as his steps, until she walked out into the light of day from the shadow of the doorway. Then his smiling eyes glanced behind her, searching the shadows for something or someone else. Rhea realised in that moment that she was not the sister he was expecting to see. *Oh, Charlotte,* Rhea thought, *what have you been doing on your rides out with Jenkins?*

'I wish to go to Mrs Delworthy's establishment,' she informed him, then walked forward and held out her gloved hand so that he could help steady her as she stepped up. Instead, he hesitated, looking at the door, his attention completely elsewhere. 'Jenkins!' she snapped the word out and saw a flash of what she could only presume was annoyance visible from those startling eyes of his as he finally acknowledged her presence. He was quite a fearsome character — or could be, she decided. Not at all like Mr Williamson. Jenkins, she decided, lacked warmth. But her father trusted him, and she trusted her father's judgement in men. Rhea therefore did not fear him, but was wary of how much liberty Charlotte had allowed him to have with her. Perhaps, Rhea thought, Charlotte had found her soulmate in life. *Queen Charlotte and the footman.* She smiled and managed to get herself up into the gig.

'Are you going to drive me to town,' she said, half in annoyance and half in amusement, 'or do I have to take the vehicle myself?'

Jenkins quickly took his seat, and soon they were moving purposefully down the drive. 'Sorry, miss,' he said. 'I thought Miss Charlotte needed the gig today.'

'Miss Charlotte is still abed. She had the gig yesterday.' Rhea did not say anything else, but looked around at the beauty of the moors as they came into view. They travelled at a decent pace, and Rhea remembered the words of her sister about enjoying the air on her face. She was correct — it was a lovely feeling, though with it came the risk of getting tanned skin. This was more likely to happen with Rhea's darker complexion, whereas Charlotte went pink and then soon paled again.

Once they were on the level ground of the moor road, Rhea decided it was a good place to ask some questions. 'Jenkins, do you know the man whom Father has invited to stay with us from Sunday?' she said as innocently as she could. Jenkins was a tall, solidly built man, and Rhea was aware of his size as she sat next to him in the gig. If Charlotte had fallen for him, she could see why he might appear attractive to her in a rough and unruly manner.

'Yes, he was one of my officers. I served under him for a year or two.'

The answer came freely enough, so Rhea persisted, despite his lips closing in a tight line. 'Was he a good officer?' she asked.

'He got the job done well enough, miss.' He glanced down at her, seemingly more relaxed and somewhat curious as to where her questions were leading.

'Would you say he is a good man, then?'

'I would say he is a good man in many ways, miss. But then … ' He looked ahead and quickened the speed slightly.

'But then what?' she asked when he had to slow again to traverse a badly rutted section.

'Sorry, miss, I was speaking out of turn,' he replied, and focused on the road ahead of them.

'It has never stopped you before.' She smiled as he shot her a quick glance. She had heard him being vocal on many a subject in the kitchens and stables before he realised she was near. It paid to slip around the Hall almost unseen, like the servants did. Charlotte and even her father seemed to forget that they also had hearts, ears and minds of their own, yet they trusted them to act like loyal mutes.

'Being a good man does not necessarily mean he is the *right* one.' Jenkins flicked the reins and the horse broke into a trot.

Rhea held on tightly. Once they had to slow again on the approach to the bridge near the Norman church in Gorebeck, the horse fell into an even gait. 'He is not the right one for what?' she asked.

He laughed. 'Not for what, miss; for whom … I will drop you off outside Mrs Delworthy's shop and then take the gig around the back to the stables. Send the lad for me when you are done. I'll be in The Hare and Rabbit.'

'Very well, Jenkins. Do not imbibe too much. I wish to return safely.' She caught his look of annoyance as she stepped down, this time with the aid of his hand to steady her, onto the pavement. He had given her orders, and she would have remind him who was in whose service. Perhaps, she wondered, Charlotte had allowed him to forget.

* * *

'Oh, I am truly blessed, as your lovely sister, Miss Charlotte, was only in here yesterday,' fawned the proprietor of the haberdashery. 'Do you wish a new set of outfits too, to see you through the season?' The woman clasped her hands together with excitement at the thought. Rhea wondered just how many dresses Charlotte had dared to order. The smile froze on her face as she saw the look of expectation on Mrs Delworthy's face. The words 'a new set of outfits' resounded in her mind. Whatever had Charlotte done? The major would have a fit of temper when he found out.

'I have come for some inspiration and advice,' Rhea said. 'I am in need of some new things for a tour I may be going on.'

'Well you have come to the right place, if I say so myself.' Mrs Delworthy smiled so widely that Rhea thought the corners of her mouth might well touch the lobes of her ears.

'Perhaps if you could show me Charlotte's choices, I could think about how to complement them with my own colouring.'

'Yes, yes of course.' Mrs Delworthy brought out the portfolios with all of Charlotte's choices collected neatly together. There were undergarments, stockings, shifts, dresses for nearly every occasion with co-ordinating spencers, and a riding coat, hat and boots. It was all Rhea could do not to let out a long gasp of disbelief. Her father's heart might not take the shock of his daughter being so bold. He could afford it, of that Rhea was sure — but would he want to, without even having been consulted? Charlotte was a determined character, but this time she had really gone too far.

Rhea asked about lighter fabrics that she would need for her trip and looked at different patterns, making mental notes of prices and choices. After an hour, she had made a few small purchases and promised to return with an order once she had been given more detail from her father regarding their future plans.

She left in good spirits, thinking there was one garment noticeably missing from Charlotte's portfolio, and that was a dress to be wed in. Whatever she was planning, a rushed marriage did not seem to be part of it.

11

Rhea was so shocked by her discoveries that she had quite forgotten to have Mrs Delworthy's boy sent to tell Jenkins she was ready to leave. Instead, she found herself walking along the pavement in a muddled daze. Charlotte was having fittings for a functional set of outfits that could be either serviceable or fanciful. Rhea was wondering which one of them it was who was planning to travel. True, Charlotte had not ordered attire suitable for travel in hot climates, but she was certainly going to be more than adequately prepared for England's varied weather. Rhea glanced over to the church and said a quick silent prayer asking for divine inspiration as to how the mess their small family was in would manage to work itself out to a happy conclusion.

'Miss Buckleby!'

The voice snapped her out of her

ponderings. Startled, she looked around to see the smiling countenance of Mr Williamson approaching her.

'I am sorry, miss,' he said. 'I did not mean to surprise you so. I am a little clumsy in my ways; I am simply more used to ordering men than approaching young ladies in the street.' He stooped in front of her and laughed. 'Apologies that did not sound quite correct either. What a mess I am making of this. I am very afraid that small talk is not my area of expertise. Could we walk along by the river for a spell and continue our conversation?' He gestured to the tow path leading away from the bridge.

'I ... ' Rhea looked at him and realised he did not see how that would send tongues wagging in such a small town as Gorebeck. Her family were known and respected, or at least she hoped so. Charlotte had most likely already set a fire kindling with her rides in the gig with Jenkins, if she had not been careful to appear proper.

The vehicle was something her father

had been loath to purchase, but was persuaded to by Charlotte after their mother's death. It was to lift her out of her grief once the period of mourning had passed, and help her face the world again. The major trusted Jenkins to see that it was used for going around the estate and the occasional journey to pay a visit to neighbours. Rhea was only too aware that he would not approve of Charlotte's more frequent trips out with Jenkins seated so comfortably at her side. What was more, he would expect Jenkins or Rhea to reveal such improper conduct to him. Rhea had thought Jenkins was her father's obedient servant, and had been unaware that she had been the silent bystander to his subterfuge as he wooed her sister. Now this man, another soldier of her father's acquaintance, wanted to walk with her on a tow path in the middle of the day. What would the townsfolk think of them?

'It wouldn't be seemly, sir,' she answered, his face fleetingly changing expression to one of disappointment before he politely responded.

'No ... pardon me for asking. I forget; I have been away from life and gentility for too long. It seems I have forgotten many things.' He stared across the river as if breathing in its peace. 'In war, things happen more immediately through necessity. Manners are a luxury.'

Rhea felt a pang of sympathy for him as she listened to his words. How many souls had been damaged by their visions of blood and death? Decorum would not have her think of such things; but the more men who returned from the wars, the more the shadow of what they had been forced to see and do hung over them and the country. Rhea realised Travis had meant no insult or harm by his invitation. He had risked his life daily for his fellow countrymen, and here she was refusing to even give him the time of day.

'I was about to buy some flowers to leave on my mother's grave,' she said. 'I often slip into the church afterwards to say a quiet prayer.' She glanced at the ancient building. It was clear to her that

Travis did not take her meaning, or was unsure she meant that he should join her there. 'It is usually empty at this hour, but you never know who you might unexpectedly meet there. Many people having pressing issues they want to pray about.'

'Indeed,' he said, with renewed hope in those deep, dark pools; how much warmer they were than Jenkins's indistinct ones, Rhea thought. 'Yes, I am overdue a visit.' He smiled. Then, as he looked over to the graveyard that surrounded the building, his countenance became more serious. 'I have many souls to pray for and sins for which I must ask forgiveness.'

'Then good day, sir,' Rhea said, and the two politely parted. Travis walked with a confident stride past the shops. She noticed how he had crossed the bridge and disappeared from sight. He had enough sense not to walk straight into the church by the main door.

She took her time buying the flowers that had been her mother's favourites — white roses; and then, as she often did, she went to her grave and left them there, removing the old ones. Even though Charlotte had always been the favourite child, the woman had been Rhea's mother, and for that she had Rhea's gratitude, if not quite the respect that she had for her father.

With a calm manner and unhurried step, Rhea made her way into the church. Pausing momentarily, she looked to the altar and admired the beauty of the Christ figure illuminated by the sunlight as it shone through the stained-glass window. It was a comforting sight.

She glanced around the church, which appeared to be empty, and made her way to the unlit candles. Saying a quick prayer, she lit one, knelt, and then found a quiet corner of a pew tucked out of sight from the main door behind one of the church's columns. There she sat and waited, wondering how long she should stay.

★　★　★

Travis watched from behind a stone arch at the back of the church as Rhea entered and silently, prayerfully, paid her respects to her dead mother and to her God. He was not sure who or what 'God' was, but his prayers on the battlefield had been answered, and so he was happy to put his faith in him. Therefore, this was the perfect place in which to follow up his instinct and learn more about this Miss Buckleby. This daughter he had taken to; the other one he had no wish to know.

He walked silently down the side of the church; he had already been around the building to make sure that it was empty. He had seen the priest enter the vicarage opposite. So for another few stolen moments he might enjoy Rhea's company.

'Miss Buckleby,' he said quietly as he approached. She had looked around as if sensing his presence. This time there was no start or look of shock at his sudden appearance. Instead she slipped elegantly along the pew so that he might sit next to her.

'Mr Williamson, you are a persistent man.' Her words were unexpectedly direct.

'When I have made a mistake, I do my best to correct it.' Travis sat on the pew, turning slightly to the side so that he could look at her fully. He rested his left arm on the back of the pew in front.

'A mistake, sir?' she asked.

'Yes; I did not know you had a sister. I presumed wrongly that you were the Miss Buckleby whom I had been asked by your father to marry.'

Her reaction was instant. She made it quite obvious that she could not read whether he was disappointed or not. 'So you were asking *me* if I carried another man's child, sir? How foolish of me not to realise what your words meant sooner.'

She sat forward, intending to stand and walk away. If that was how she thought he regarded her, then her reaction was not surprising. Travis had to stifle a grin, for his way with women — gentlewomen — was lacking.

'Please.' He put his hand on her elbow.

Rhea stared at him, and then looked purposefully down at his hand, as he had stopped her from rising.

'I apologise.' He removed his hand. 'I meant that I wished to know why I had been so urgently summoned to marry the major's daughter. The letter did not state he had more than one, or if there was a pressing reason for the request. What was I to think? Any man would have his suspicions in such a situation; especially when the father is a high-ranking officer of position, and his daughter is so attractive.'

'Well, you could have taken the suggestion as a compliment — that he valued you as a person and wanted you to be his son-in-law!' Rhea snapped out her words in a more abrupt manner than she had intended to.

'I could have; but when the letter arrived I was not at my best, and therefore ... ' He realised he had nearly admitted that he had been in Newgate prison. What dread that would have filled this lady's heart with if he had.

'You were not at your best?' He had her full attention now. It was as if she sensed the truth, so he decided to confide a part of it to her.

'I returned to discover that my father had died three months earlier, but I had not been told. Letters must have gone astray ... ' He allowed his words to drift off as he watched her reaction.

'I'm so sorry. No wonder Father thought of you as a match. You must have been devastated.'

'I was. And, worse still, our family home had been sold by my elder brother without my knowledge. So you see, the life and home I fought for had simply disappeared.'

Her attention was absolute. Travis could sense her empathy for his situation as she placed her gloved hand upon his. This single tender gesture was more than anyone had genuinely shared with him in years. He looked at her hand, so small and delicate compared to his. If he were a cad, this lady would be putty in his hands. But he was not, and so he shook his head and looked at her lovely face. There would be nothing but honesty between them. If he expected her to be so with him, then he had to show her trust also.

'Miss Buckleby, I behaved badly when I returned to London. I drank my sorrow away, as I was lonely, desperate and confused. I had seen men — friends and enemies — die on battlefields. To get through the darkness, I had filled my heart with the joy of returning home and making my father proud. I am a second son, and as such I never expected to inherit the estate; but to have lost him and my home in such a way was a shock beyond those I had endured while I served. My purpose, my hope and my heart all broke.'

He had to pause to swallow. This dear lady's eyes were bringing out of him words that he had never spoken to another mortal. With them flowed emotions he had tried to drink away. 'I was foolish,' he continued. 'I gave in to provocation and got myself into a fight. A mutual friend sent word to the major, and I was released from the lock-up once his letter and funds were received. Your father saved my skin for the second time. The first was on a battlefield, where he stopped a Corsair from parting my head from my arrogant younger shoulders. So you have the truth of it. This is a place for confession and truth, is it not? I owe him everything, but all I ask is that before I honour my debt, I at least understand fully the reason for his request.'

Still holding his hand, Rhea nodded. 'I do not know any real reason,' she replied, 'other than that Charlotte is headstrong and has upset Father with her foolish words on many an occasion. She was spoilt by Mother; and since her death, Charlotte has become quite outspoken. Father fears she would not do well should she come out in the season, and would have her set with a husband who can mould her into the woman she should truly be: a good wife and, in time, a mother.' Now it was she who swallowed.

'So I am to create a good wife from a reluctant bride. How so?' Travis stood up and looked at the column next to him.

'Kindly, I hope, Mr Williamson. She is not really a bad person; just opinionated.' She had edged to the end of the pew and was watching Travis as he spun around to face her.

'I am not a brute, miss. I would not beat a woman — any woman — to make her do my will. But your sister has no wish to be my wife.' He saw her curiosity rise.

'You have met her?' she asked.

'Our paths crossed yesterday, when she was in the gig with my ex-sergeant, Jenkins.'

'Goodness. You have made excellent use of your time, sir. Tell me — before you are officially due to meet either of us, is there anything else you would know? It seems that in your haste to attend before you were invited, you have inadvertently made a right mess of things.' She raised a challenging eyebrow, and he bit back his immediate response, for it would not be fitting for a young maid to hear it.

'In the last two days,' he said, 'your sister has nearly ploughed me into the pavement and run me into the dale with that gig of hers. She is wild. She has little grace to her manner, and her eyes are those of a tiger. Do I like a challenge? Yes. Do I want to fight any more battles? No. Do I wish to wed such an unruly, petulant child? Also, no. For she has none of your grace and intelligence, and I would never be able to trust her.' He stopped for breath, cursing himself silently, despite his surroundings, for allowing his words to flow freely like water from a great height.

'Oh, Mr Williamson, you are no match for Charlotte.' Rhea grinned and stood up. 'Her words flow with equal heat and passion to yours. She needs a man who can hold his own and out-think her. To her, you would be nothing but an obstacle to overcome. No, I am certain that the pair of you are not suited; but Father is determined, and he is also used to having his way. So we must think fast, because he returns in two days; and unless a solution is found, we will be faced with a situation of charades that can only end badly.' She looked at him and smiled, curling only one side of her mouth up in an unusual yet appealing manner. 'My grace and intelligence,' she repeated, and he noticed her colouring heighten slightly.

'Yes, Miss Buckleby; that is what I said, and that is what I meant. I have been brought here to proposition the wrong sister. I believe we would have far more in common.'

He watched her eyes stare up into his. Her face moved with emotion. She was easy for him to read; her eyes showed honesty. If he had not been standing in a house of God, and was not worried about scaring her away, he would have placed his lips over hers and showed her just how they could be right for each other. No words were spoken between them for a moment; but as Travis's eyes looked longingly at Rhea's lips, he noticed hers doing likewise.

The moment was broken when she glanced at the double doors. 'I must leave, as Jenkins will wonder where I have got to.' She licked those lovely red lips, and

Travis wished he could dispense with everything society thought proper and embrace her there and then. But that he could not do, for he would hate to frighten her or break the nascent bond between them.

'Jenkins,' he said. 'He was my sergeant. I saw Charlotte leaning into him on the gig; she seemed very happy in his company.'

Rhea did not look back at him. 'I must be on my way, but thank you for being so honest with me. I will give thought to your words and predicament and would ask you to do the same. Tomorrow, if the weather is fine, I shall no doubt ride to the oak wood on the edge of our estate. There is a folly hidden amongst the trees that I like to read in, normally on a morning ... about the hour of ten.'

'Good day, miss,' Travis said, and watched her walk out into the daylight, leaving him to sit and ponder and pray a while. Yet, tomorrow was another day. He smiled.

12

Charlotte awoke and summoned her maid, Judd. The girl seemed distracted.

'Tell Jenkins I will need the gig again today. I forgot to order something in town.'

'Sorry, miss. He can't come today because Miss Rhea decided to go out, and he is with her.' The girl drew back the curtains and the bright sunshine flooded the room. It was a beautifully sunny day, which vexed Charlotte. She would be stuck in the Hall when she could have been riding with Jenkins.

'I'll go and fetch your things, miss.' Before Charlotte could ask her why she wasn't seeing to her there and then, Judd disappeared.

She flopped back on her bed, and must have cat-napped for another twenty minutes or so; certainly time had gone by. Yet there was no sign of her maid, her clothes, or a pitcher of warm water on her washstand. Charlotte had a strange feeling that something was very wrong, but she could not fathom what it was.

She opened her bedchamber door and shouted 'Judd! Donaldson!' at the top of her voice, but there was no response. Puzzled, she pulled the bell cord and shouted again for her maid. After some twenty minutes, the girl finally arrived at her bedchamber doorway. She looked flushed, as though she had been running.

'Judd, where have you been? Where is everyone today? I want hot water to wash in and my clothes laid out, and I want you to do my hair. You have been here long enough to know my morning routine. My breakfast should be made ready, and then I would have Mrs Donaldson attend me, as I have work for her to do. Where is that woman?'

Charlotte stopped mid-tirade, as the girl looked as if she was about to break down. Her eyes were those of a frightened rabbit, and she had clearly been crying. 'What is it, Judd? Is something badly amiss?' Charlotte's change in tone from anger to sympathy was enough for the girl to buckle. Tears ran down her cheeks. 'Tell me. If it is that bad, I think I need to know, don't you?' Charlotte had swallowed back her own temper as curiosity overwhelmed her. It was rare that something interrupted the routines her father had instilled in the servants, so what had caused such a disruption this morning?

The girl nodded. 'It's Mrs Donaldson, miss. Her baby has come early,' she whispered, and sniffed.

Charlotte stood up. Surely she had misheard what Judd had said. 'Her baby?' she repeated.

'Yes, miss. Her baby has arrived early.' Judd could not look Charlotte in the eye.

'Were you aware that Mrs Donaldson was expecting a child?' Charlotte asked, and saw the girl anxiously shake her head.

So that was why the housekeeper was always so anxious. Her dress hung on her because she was wearing a loose gown so that her bulge was hidden or disguised.

Charlotte breathed deeply. She needed to think quickly. Her father would have the woman thrown out, child and all, for this. Yes, she was called 'Mrs', but she was a widow, and her husband was no father to this child.

Charlotte grabbed a robe from the peg behind her door and wrapped herself in it. She slid her feet into her slippers and quickly brushed out her hair, using a ribbon to tie back its volume and pins to keep it in place. 'Take me to her,' she said.

The girl was almost shaking with either fear or distress, so Charlotte said kindly, 'Now, please,' rather than barking another command in her face.

They walked briskly into the servants' quarters along a plain corridor to a room at the end. Charlotte had never been in this part of the house, and as she looked around at the plain walls and floor devoid of even low-quality carpeting, she thought that if she was to be mistress of the Hall, things were going to change. Surely her father could afford some carpet for them.

After all, the servants walked up and down it enough.

Discreetly she swallowed while Judd turned the handle and opened the door to Mrs Donaldson's room. Stepping inside, Charlotte saw the now even paler woman lying in the bed and holding a small bundle in front of her wrapped in a piece of sheeting. The day was warm and the room stuffy.

'Open the window a crack and let the poor thing breathe,' Charlotte said to Judd. 'Does anyone else know of this?' she asked the older woman as she pulled back the cloth that was wrapped around the tiny baby's face. It was small, had a full head of dark hair, and looked healthy in colour. The hair ruled out Jenkins as the father, as his was fair to ginger. The thought pleased Charlotte. She surprised herself for even considering it, but he was hers, and she would not have taken kindly to him if he had been having an affair.

'Cook,' the maid said as she allowed some fresh air in.

'Judd, go to Cook then, and tell her that I wish her to make whatever broth or meal is best for a new mother and whatever the baby needs. Use the best ingredients, for Mrs Donaldson looks in need of a good meal, and she can hardly feed her child if she is ill herself. If no one else knows, then just tell the dairy maids and staff that she is unwell. No more is to be said for now, unless this little bundle screams the Hall down.'

She stared at the tired, drawn face of the woman lying in the bed, clinging to her precious bundle, but her mind was racing. Once the maid had gone, Charlotte sat down on the hard wooden chair, which was the only furniture in the room other than the bed, drawers, chest and small table. 'Is it a girl or a boy?' she asked.

'He is a boy child,' the woman answered quite clearly.

'Is he well?'

'Yes; just a little small because he has come early, but he is perfect.'

Charlotte thought that while Mrs

Donaldson may be worn out, there was a spark in her voice which was not there before. Defiance, or pride? Charlotte wondered. If it was pride, then it had ironically arrived after this woman's fall. How strange, she thought, that this wisp of a woman was at her mercy and charity, and yet here she was staring at Charlotte directly not hours after giving her bastard breath.

'Who is the father?' Charlotte asked, and watched Mrs Donaldson stare down at her child, but she did not speak. 'My father returns soon. He will need to know, and it will be the first question on his lips. If you tell me, I will send word and have the man take responsibility for this life.'

Mrs Donaldson shook her head. 'No word can be sent. When your father returns, then I will tell him.' She still did not look up.

Charlotte wondered if she had been given something that had dulled her wits. Her father might choose not to even set eyes upon either of them. If he could marry off his eldest daughter to a halfwit, then he was certainly capable of casting a ruined servant and her brat from his estate. She would have to fall upon the charity of the parish if that happened, unless she had a relative with a very accommodating heart willing to take them in.

'Very well,' Charlotte said as she stood up. 'But, Mrs Donaldson, he has a poor temper, and he will not look kindly upon this.'

'Why are you?' Mrs Donaldson asked, and this time her tired eyes found Charlotte's curious ones.

'Why am I what?' Charlotte said, taken aback by being asked a question without due address as the mistress. Did childbirth turn the meek into mother dragons? she wondered.

'Why are you being kind to me, then? You never have been before now; and you, too, are known for your quick temper.'

Charlotte wondered if this woman had resigned herself to her fate and had thrown caution and sense to the wind.

How dare any servant, particularly one who had just given birth to an illegitimate child and was living by her mistress's goodwill, are to question her so? Yet Charlotte smiled. She had never paid the woman any attention before because she was an insipid puppy who obeyed her father's whims. And yet here she was, being calm, collected and defiant.

'Take care, *Mrs* Donaldson. You have a young life dependent upon the goodwill of others. Do not try and criticise me, or you may discover that kindness is ephemeral and can disappear with that quick temper you are so keen to question.' Charlotte turned to leave her to her thoughts.

'Miss Charlotte, I did not seek to question your temper, but merely to ask why, when I know it so well, it has not shown itself when I am plainly at your mercy until your father returns.'

Charlotte shook her head and glanced back at the woman. 'Perhaps I am not as bad as people apparently think I am,' she offered; for in truth she really did not know the reason herself. Then her eyes noticed something else that completely distracted her attention. A stain was forming on the blanket. She swallowed. 'Cook!' she shouted.

The woman appeared. She and Judd had obviously been near at hand in case all hell broke loose and Charlotte's infamous temper ran riot in the poor woman's room.

'Judd, go to the stables and have the boy Samuel fetch Dr Sanderson. Tell him I need him urgently, and no more. He will come quickly if he thinks I am ailing. Cook, come — we need your help.'

Charlotte ran to Mrs Donaldson's bedside and scooped the baby into her arms. His mother had drifted off into what appeared to be a deep sleep.

'What do we do?' Charlotte looked at the stain on the blanket.

'I'll do what I can,' Cook said. 'You put that little one in that drawer.' Charlotte could see that they had made a makeshift cot from an empty drawer lined with an old blanket. 'When Judd returns, get yourself presentable for when the doctor arrives. And say your prayers. She is so thin, miss ... but she's a tough one.'

13

Travis sat a while and pondered how he would address the major. He needed to convey his willingness to answer his call, but then refuse to offer for the hand of the elder sister. It was going to require tact; and that, he thought with a smile, was something he seemed to have forgotten over the last few years.

* * *

Rhea returned to Mrs Delworthy's establishment in a very contemplative mood, and asked that her boy be sent to fetch Jenkins. It was as Jenkins pulled the gig up to the raised pavement outside the shop that the stable lad, Samuel, appeared riding one of the estate's horses. He seemed fixed on where he was going and did not acknowledge Rhea's presence at first.

Jenkins shouted to the lad as he pulled his horse to a stop alongside them. 'What are you doing here, boy?' he asked before Rhea had a chance to speak.

'I am here to fetch Dr Sanderson to the Hall, sir.' The lad steadied his horse, which had obviously been going at a gallop.

'Why? What's happened?' Rhea said. 'Who needs the doctor?'

The boy looked worried. 'Miss, I was told that I was to fetch the doctor quick as I could, as Miss Charlotte wanted him.'

'Go!' Jenkins ordered, as he spun around the gig and helped Rhea up. 'Hold on, miss,' he instructed her as he made his way at speed back to the Hall.

* * *

Travis was riding out of the stable yard as the doctor and Samuel were just arriving to fetch the doctor's horse.

'Good day, sir,' Travis said. He could see the urgency in the man as he nodded quickly, eager to be past him.

130

'I must hurry.' The doctor mounted his horse after fastening his bag securely to the saddle.

'Do you need any help? Has something happened?' Travis asked, his soldier's instinct kicking in. 'I have tended the wounded before when in the field.'

'Miss Buckleby is taken ill, sir. Excuse me; I must be on my way. I doubt it will be from a battle injury,' Dr Sanderson said dismissively, and rode out into the street.

Travis was not going to be deterred so easily, and so he rode with them. His thoughts were in even more of a turmoil as he pondered a possibility that had never crossed his mind before — that Charlotte was in fact ailing. And here he was, judging her poorly.

★   ★   ★

Rhea was jolted and shaken as, in his keenness to return to the Hall, Jenkins's driving had become erratic. His haste, she thought, was going to see them in need of the good doctor's care. Her request to slow down was lost on the wind as they gathered speed. Only necessity brought him to his senses as he traversed the steep descent and bend as they made their way from the moor road to the vale.

Rhea wondered if Mr Williamson's presumption about Charlotte's condition was true. What if the infatuation with their footman had been more than that? It did not bear thinking about. But why else would Charlotte become so suddenly ill? Then Rhea remembered the way her mother had pampered her sister because she had been a sickly child. Guilt played with concern as they approached.

Rhea was helped down from the gig by a very agitated Jenkins as they stopped outside the Hall's door. She ran through the entrance, and he followed close at her heels. They both stood stock still as Charlotte greeted them, looking more than a little bemused by the manner of their approach.

'You are well, Charlotte! Thank God!' Jenkins exclaimed as he stepped in front of Rhea, who thought he was about to embrace her sister. But Charlotte placed a hand on his chest and walked around him to Rhea.

'Charlotte, whatever is wrong?' Rhea asked. 'Why send for a doctor?'

Charlotte shook her head. 'You care so much, little sister,' she said, and stroked Rhea's cheek with her finger.

'Of course I do. Why have you sent for the doctor?' Rhea repeated, but Jenkins was already looking back out of the doors as three riders appeared: the doctor, Samuel and Travis.

'Mrs Donaldson is in need of help,' Charlotte said. 'I will explain later. Calm yourselves, as I see to the doctor. Jenkins, please tend to the horses. I assure you, I am quite well.' She smiled as he nodded. Seemingly satisfied, he left them to it.

'Rhea,' Charlotte continued, 'perhaps you could entertain Mr Williamson while I take the doctor to see his patient. I will explain later, for there is much to share.'

Rhea wondered what she had been missing, as her sister had surprised her with what appeared to be yet another change of manner. If this one was genuine, Rhea had to admit she much preferred it.

'Doctor, please come with me.' Without further explanation, Charlotte led Dr Sanderson away.

Rhea caught sight of Judd coming out of the servants' stairway. 'Judd, please come with me.' The girl looked anxiously back at her.

Travis had arrived in the hallway just in time to see Charlotte disappearing with the doctor. 'She still walks, then?' he asked.

Rhea was uncertain if he was being observational or sarcastic. 'Please, will you wait in the library for me? I will join you shortly.' She showed him to the doorway.

'It appears I have presented myself again at an inopportune moment, but I feared that something serious had befallen your sister. I wished only to offer you my support.'

'I thought the same, but it appears we have both jumped to the wrong conclusion. However, I feel there is something serious afoot, and I would know what. Please be patient and make yourself at home,' she said.

He raised an eyebrow when she used the word 'home', but she ignored the gesture as she was in no mood for wit of any kind. 'Judd, a moment!' she called. The young maid followed her into the morning room, where Rhea shut the doors behind her. 'Now, tell me what is happening here. I want the honest truth.'

Rhea listened in disbelief. So the edgy, anxious Mrs Donaldson had been with child. No wonder her clothes were loose-fitting; that she had been acting more and more ill at ease when she had to face people; and that she'd wanted to hide behind her household chores and stay out of sight of curious eyes.

'But how? Her husband died over a year ago. So who was the father?' Rhea blurted out the words and saw Judd look down. Her eyes could not meet Rhea's.

'She will not say,' Judd stated, but did not look up.

'Do you know or have suspicions, Judd? If so, I would have you tell me, for he has a young life to support.' Rhea watched the top of the girl's head as she shook it, still staring at her feet.

'You know, don't you?' Rhea persisted.

'Miss, please don't. I need this job. It's none of my business.' She began to sob.

14

Nearly an hour later, Charlotte escorted the doctor to the morning room, where tea had been prepared for him. She had expected to find Rhea waiting there, but the room was empty, as Rhea had joined Travis in the library.

Once inside, Charlotte composed herself while she asked, 'Will she survive?' She hoped she could cope with events if the answer was negative, but she had to know. Her world had become so strange to her. From thinking daily about what was to fill the long hours ahead of her, and increasingly plotting to see if she could spend some in the company of Jenkins, she now found her time filled by dealing with matters of life and death. Should she be ashamed to admit that she actually enjoyed thinking beyond her own needs?

Dr Sanderson placed his bag on the

table by the fire and considered his answer as he stared into the dying flames. Charlotte watched his greying hairline rise as he expressed his thoughts. He was a handsome man of maturing years, yet he still stood straight, and had the strong frame of a man who had looked after himself well over a lifetime.

'I would prefer to address such weighty matters to your father, Miss Charlotte. It is hardly a subject a young lady should be dealing with on her own. Perhaps you would like your sister to be with you, as he is not here? Perhaps you would like Miss Rhea to sit with you a while? You have had quite a shock already.'

Charlotte realised he was phrasing his words very carefully. She could feel her temper rise. How dare he talk to her, after all she had faced in the last few hours, as if she had no knowledge of the world?

'I sent for you, sir, because I am dealing with a difficult situation. Can you please answer my question, and not defer to others who have not as yet been informed of the details? I promise I will not faint. And if I do, then I am sure you have something suitable that would bring me around in that fine bag of yours.' She smiled politely to try and soften her outspoken sarcasm.

She was surprised when the doctor nodded as if he agreed with her comments. He even looked as if he approved of her bold words.

'Very well, I shall give you my verdict. If the fever breaks this night, then she stands a good chance of making a full recovery. She is weak and will need care. This is no malady; this is a loss of blood — which, thank God, has abated. But if she is moved, it may start again.

'She has also been carrying a heavy burden of shame within her body. I do not think I need state the obvious — that if the major seeks to dismiss her, deciding to turn her out, then the answer is simply no, she will not survive.

'The child is in good health, if not a little small, as he seems to have been a bit too eager to join our troubled world. If he is not nurtured and nourished, it will be the death of him also.' He shrugged his shoulders. 'Life is often harsh for those who break with morality.'

Charlotte bristled. 'She will not be turned out. I will see to it that she is given care and that the child stays nearby. No baby should be ripped from its mother's side. I will personally guarantee this. I will not be her judge! I do not have all the facts.'

Her words came out with a natural conviction of passion. The doctor was watching her with a slightly surprised expression upon his face. Was her character so badly thought of, she wondered, that he would think her capable of seeing a mother removed from her sick bed and cast out into the world? Was the doctor so shocked that she should be forgiving of the woman who lay abed fighting for her life?

At that moment she saw her discarded embroidery on the chair near the window, and could not but smile at it as she remembered how her temper had snapped in a petulant fit only days before. How long ago it seemed that she was throwing it down in the heat of a childish tantrum. So what had changed? Looking at the doctor's face, she supposed the answer was herself. But why? Well that was a question yet to be answered, even by her.

'I cannot condone such a situation,' Dr Sanderson commented. 'Morally it is beyond acceptable; and you should be nowhere near her, Miss Charlotte. But I would not have her die for it. I will leave you these drops and suggest she be allowed to have bed rest for a week at least. Once she is fit, she can answer for her failings, and your father will no doubt decide what is to be done with her and the child. You can have complete trust in my discretion. No word of this will reach town from me. I do not wish any shame to fall upon your good household and family name.'

'That is very considerate of you, Dr Sanderson. I will inform my father on his return. Thank you for coming so quickly.' Charlotte offered him his tea, but was anxious to see him leave.

Rhea heard the door being shut as the doctor left, and immediately sought Charlotte out. 'Is she ... will she be all right?' she asked. 'And the baby?'

'The mother is resting, while the child is being lulled to sleep by Cook,' Charlotte said. 'Dinner will be late today.'

'That is the least of our concerns. You look very tired,' Rhea remarked.

Charlotte turned to the doorway as Travis appeared there. 'Mr Williamson, you must stay for dinner. I am grateful for you escorting my sister back in our little time of crisis.' She was the essence of politeness.

Travis stepped into the room. 'What exactly is the crisis, if I may be so bold as to ask? For whatever it is, if I can help you — either of you — I will.'

Rhea saw Charlotte smile and was eager that her old temper did not spark off now; not as everything in their world was somehow changing yet again. 'Please tell us if she will be all right, Charlotte, whatever it is that ails her?' Rhea asked.

'I believe that she will be fine once the night has passed, but it may be a long one for us all as we wait to see the outcome. However, we will need to make sure her baby is kept warm and well also, for it is on the small side.'

'Her baby?' Travis repeated.

'Yes,' Charlotte said. 'The emergency concerns our housekeeper, Mrs Donaldson, who has just given birth. It is already late in the afternoon. Could I suggest you join us for dinner?' she offered.

'No, but thank you,' Travis answered. 'I can see you have much to occupy yourselves. I will ride back in the morning if I may, and make sure all is well.' He looked at Rhea, but it was Charlotte who responded.

'Mr Williamson, under the circumstances may I suggest that you stay here tonight, seeing as how you were intending to visit from tomorrow onwards anyway. Then tomorrow morning you can go and collect your things in the gig and return.

By then we will know if Mrs Donaldson has come through the fever, or if our crisis has become a tragedy. Besides, Father will be returning sometime during the day, and we all have much to talk to him about, do we not?'

Rhea was amazed to see Charlotte reacting in such a calm manner.

'Very well, and thank you for your hospitality,' Travis said. He left with Judd, who showed him to the room that had been prepared for his stay.

★　★　★

Rhea saw Charlotte watching him go. 'He will make someone a fine husband, Rhea, but not me I am afraid. Was that what you wished to tell me yesterday when I cut you short? Did you wish to tell me I should abide by Father's decision for the good of all?' Charlotte's voice was calm as she posed her question.

Rhea stared at her. 'No. It is not my place to do that, for your life is yours to live. You will have to find a way of persuading Father to see this. Mr Williamson called, that is what I wanted to tell you.' Rhea stared at her and Charlotte nodded.

'Then I should have listened to you instead of putting you down, as I have a tendency to.' She gave a tired, impish smile. 'I apologise unreservedly for my high-handedness.'

Rhea was delighted to hear the words. 'Perhaps. You have changed in some way, have you not?'

'Perhaps it is about time that I did.' She looped her hand through the cusp of Rhea's arm and walked her to the door.

'Is Jenkins the father, Charlotte? I confronted Judd, who I am sure knows the truth, but refuses to admit it. Jenkins and Mrs Donaldson spend quite a lot of time together.' Rhea half-expected the question to snap Charlotte's pretence, if that was indeed what it was.

'Absolutely not! I am in no doubt of that. Come, little sister — I will show you a delightful little child. And you can say your prayers for his mother, for indeed she needs some, and I believe yours may be better practised than mine, my dear Rhea.'

Rhea laughed out loud. She was unsure how anyone could change so quickly and seemingly sincerely.

15

Rhea looked at the tiny baby in her arms and could not believe that this scaled-down version of humanity could still be healthy. Yet it cried heartily: the little mouth opened like a mini-chasm, and out of it came a grating shriek of a cry. Fortunately, the wife of an estate worker who had given birth two months earlier had agreed to be its wet nurse, and so the young babe had begun feeding and slept peacefully.

Meanwhile, his mother lay drenched in sweat nearby. The maids kept her as dry, clean and comfortable as possible, and her fitfulness seemed to have abated. If this meant the fever was subsiding, then there could be cause for celebration; but they feared that it might only mean her vigour was fading. They did not know which, but Rhea prayed heartily that night.

'If you are certain it is not Jenkins, then who could the father be?' Rhea asked Charlotte, ignoring the bristle in her sister's manner when she referred to Jenkins in such a way again.

'It cannot be him. He is different in colouring; and besides, he would not behave so dishonourably.'

Rhea resisted the urge to smile, as Charlotte obviously had feelings for their footman. Then she felt a tinge of sadness and regret, for her father would never sanction such a match.

'She does go into town every Thursday afternoon, and so could have been having a tryst with someone there.' Charlotte shrugged. 'Goodness knows. The woman is so quiet and mouse-like. No wonder she behaved like she was being followed by a ghost. It could be the butcher, the baker or the candlestick-maker — you pick.'

Rhea shook her head. 'Mrs Donaldson is no common woman. She would not behave so with just anyone. It has to be someone she loves, and that means a long liaison. If she had been attacked, we would have known when it happened, for she would not have been able to hide her upset from us.'

'Well there *is* someone, but you will not like my suggestion,' Charlotte said as she gazed at the baby.

'Who? If you know something, then share it with me.'

'Well, when she goes to church, Mr Trimble, the curate, always finds time to chat with her after the service; and he has a head of strikingly handsome dark hair and features — '

'Charlotte!' Rhea was amazed that her sister would imply such a thing. 'I can see how you entertain yourself in the services,' she chastised; but she also laughed inside, as she, too had noticed him.

'Rhea, I told you that you would not care for my thoughts, but it has to be someone she sees regularly. She does not have anyone close to her in the house, other than Jenkins; so whoever he is, he must reside in town, and be someone she has known for some time and whom she trusts. If it is Mr Trimble, Father will make him wed her or have him disgraced. He would never serve a parish again if he turns from his duty.'

Rhea looked down at the woman who paled in the bed before her. 'I fear she is losing the battle. I wish there was something I could do to make her fight for this life.'

'You are not God, Rhea. Perhaps we should summon Mr Trimble and see if he can bring her back to us.'

'If our assumption was wrong, we would only complicate things further for her and Father.' Rhea looked at the makeshift cot as the baby began to cry.

'Take the little one away,' Charlotte told her. 'She needs to rest. At least we can allow her to be at peace.'

'No! Charlotte, you are wrong. Rest and stillness may be the end of her. She needs a reason to fight back.' Rhea scooped the little one up into her arms and carefully laid him beside his mother. Tenderly she placed Mrs Donaldson's arm around him. When she was happy that he was nestled and secure, she then crouched at the side of the bed to make sure that the child was safe and could not fall off.

Together, the sisters watched while momentarily the mother's eyelids fluttered open as the baby's cry continued. Mrs Donaldson moved her arm ever so slightly and tried to hug the child to her. Rhea helped to support both the arm and the small, precious bundle it cradled. Then the child seemed to settle. Rhea looked at Mrs Donaldson's face and saw tired eyes staring back at her. 'Thank you,' she mouthed.

Rhea could feel tears well up behind her eyes, but she held them back. She was very weak, and a long way from being safe, but now there was hope. 'You need to drink and possibly try some broth, Mrs Donaldson,' she said, and the woman nodded.

The sisters stayed with her for the next hour as she sipped, replacing some much-needed nourishment, and then cuddled her baby again. When both mother and baby were ready for sleep, they left. A grateful smile was all that passed between them, as somehow they seemed to have bonded in that room in a way they had never done before. They walked along the servants' corridor that led to the hall.

'Well, this is going to be one hell of a homecoming for Father,' Charlotte said, and laughed at Rhea's pretend look of disapproval. 'Oh, little sister, it is just a place — even mentioned frequently in the Bible, I recall. It is not a swear word!' she said playfully.

'Whatever it is, it is not what a young lady should be saying!' a male voice said sternly as they stepped into the entrance hall.

'Father!' Rhea exclaimed, for once looking anything but pleased to see him standing there.

He in turn was staring at his two daughters and seemingly taking in the state of the pair of them. Neither of them were what could be called presentably turned out. Charlotte had one of

Cook's aprons around her skirts, and their hair was far from perfect. The major had high standards, and the sisters exchanged glances, knowing he would not be pleased.

'I see my presence has been sorely missed. What, pray, do you call this shambles of an appearance, Rhea? And why should either of you be returning from the servants' quarters? Take that ridiculous thing off, Charlotte; you are not the damned maid!' He pointed to the apron. Then he angrily removed his riding coat and threw it over Judd's outstretched arms. She had heard his voice and run into the entrance hall.

'Well, it is … I mean … ' Rhea's words failed her; and she, for once, looked to Charlotte for inspiration.

'How lovely to see you return, Father,' Charlotte chipped in, and smiled. 'You must be thirsty. Judd, see that some tea and refreshments are brought into the day room — for we have much to tell you, Father.' Her manner was calm, but she looked as tired as Rhea felt.

The major stormed into the day room, to be followed quickly by both of his daughters, neither at ease.

16

'Send Mrs Donaldson to me immediately,' Francis commanded. 'I would know from her what has been going on here in my absence. Why are those flowers fading and not yet replaced?' He pointed to some roses from the garden. Mrs Donaldson always kept a vase of his favourite blooms fresh when they were in flower. The sad versions that were now exhibited there were a clear sign that the woman was not well, or had not been attending to her duties.

Once the doors were closed behind them, the two sisters stared at their father, who peered back at them with a very grim countenance.

'I left you here with clear instructions to Jenkins and Donaldson to keep the house running smoothly, yet I return to see you both looking dishevelled and the place neglected. So what excuses are you conjuring up in that wilful head of yours, Charlotte?' He glared at his eldest, but as she was about to speak he also shot an angry look at Rhea. 'I am very disappointed that you would allow her to get the upper hand here.'

'Father, you judge us both ill!' Rhea replied. Charlotte's colour was high. Rhea wondered if she was about to revert to her normal type. In the short time that Charlotte had been changed, Rhea had appreciated the sister she had always hoped was still there. They had played so well as children together. It was as they turned into very different young women that the gap had formed, encouraged by their own mother.

'No!' Charlotte exclaimed. 'You will not do this, Father. You wonder why I behave badly — yes, I admit it — yet you always blame and seek to put my character down, even when I try to act as you wish me to. It is true that I dreamed of being the lady of a grand house. Most young ladies do, do they not? Is it not what is expected of us? I wanted to have everything that was supposed to make my world complete. Then Mother died and I was left with you two. Rhea looks like you, acts like you, reads like you — how was I to compete with her?'

Rhea felt sad for not realising that her sister was finding it hard to be the outsider, when she herself knew what that had felt like when her father was away being a soldier and she was left with Mother and Charlotte. The only difference was that she escaped into books, while Charlotte escaped in a gig — with Jenkins.

'You talk nonsense, child. You are my daughter also, and I love you as much as Rhea. But you always fight me.' The major stood awkwardly in front of the large mantelpiece.

'Do you?' Charlotte raised her voice, but did not shout as she normally would.

'Yes; that is why, when I was presented with a copy of a quote for a substantial order of finery from Mrs Delworthy on my return to town, I instructed her to go ahead and fulfil it — despite being enraged that you had the audacity to place such an order without my permission!' His face showed that he was livid. 'It proved what a selfish and inconsiderate, spoilt child you are. Did you even order one thing for your sister, or question whether the funds you were committing could be afforded?'

Charlotte's eyes watered. 'I apologise. I wanted to strike back at you for trading me off to one of your soldiers without even discussing the matter with me first. I wanted to choose my own husband, Father. I wanted to have a say in my own life's future. Is that so wrong?' Her eyes, tired and watery, appealed to him in a more genuine, personal way than Rhea had ever seen before. She found she understood Charlotte's actions now, even if she did not agree with them.

'I am your father. I chose wisely for you. Do you not trust my judgement?' he asked, his palms open as if imploring her to say yes without question.

'Mr Williamson is a very personable and attractive man, but he is not for me,' she answered calmly. 'Would you wish to spend your life with a woman who was 'personable', but with whom you had nothing in common, or with whom there was no spark?'

'A woman need not be 'attracted'. How do you talk so? Your duty is to make your husband's home a happy and content place in which to raise your children. What more could a woman wish for? Furthermore, how is it that you know of him? He will not arrive here until Sunday.' The major was clearly puzzled, but now both his daughters were trying to control their words and feelings, as neither agreed with his thoughts. They both wanted more, but different things.

He looked to Rhea, who said, 'He is already here, Father. I have met him on a few occasions, and Charlotte has briefly. He seems a very … a gentleman.' Rhea saw the major blink. She wanted to rush in and say that she would consider marrying him herself, and that her father could then release Charlotte to follow her own heart; but she decided that such a discussion should be had in a calmer moment.

'I have been away for only a few days, and it seems like my home fell into turmoil the minute I left!' Francis exclaimed. 'If this is not proof that both of you need a man at your side to lead you through this world, then I do not know what is. Where is Donaldson, and where is Williamson now?' He looked around as if Travis was going to appear in front of him in the doorway.

'He is upstairs,' Charlotte said, 'in the Willow Room. I asked him to stay the night, as he followed us back from town. It seemed the least we could do under the circumstances.'

The major slowly turned his head, looking from one daughter to the other, and Rhea knew that the guilty secret they had not as yet decided how to tell their father was about to be revealed.

'Mrs Donaldson is ill, Father,' Rhea explained. 'That is why we are not neat and tidy. We have been with her for hours, and … well … '

Both women locked eyes as their father's previously high colour seemed to pale slightly. 'What do you mean, ill? Why would you be with her? How ill? What has this got to do with Williamson? Has Dr Sanderson seen her? Does she have a contagion?' He raked his hand through his short hair as if trying to make sense of what he was hearing.

Charlotte cupped his elbow with her hand. 'Perhaps you had better sit down, Father,' she said, 'and then we can explain her condition to you in a calmer way.' But before she could, the door opened and Travis walked in.

'I am no old maid,' Francis grumbled. 'I commanded battles, for goodness sake. Why would I need to sit down?'

'Major Buckleby,' Travis said with enthusiasm, and strode over to shake his ex-commander's hand. 'I arrived earlier today amidst all the excitement, and am so grateful to your lovely daughters for extending their hospitality to me.' He smiled as the major's silent, bewildered appearance told everyone that this had not been the correct time to burst in upon his hosts. Rhea and Charlotte were staring at him blankly and said nothing, as the major froze at the mention of 'the excitement'.

'Travis, will you please report to me what has happened? For these women make no sense at all.' He pulled his arm free of Charlotte, not seeing the hurt in her eyes as she cast her glance downwards.

Rhea was about to round on her father and berate him for his high-handedness, for once giving way to her outrage at the way he was treating them. Yet she also realised they had failed to handle the situation well, and his wishes were in accordance with what was expected of them by society.

Travis spoke up. 'Major, your daughters have been strong in your absence. I admire both of them very much. When events could have so easily overtaken them, they have remained calm and worked together to possibly save two lives. So I think they deserve the opportunity to explain to you what has happened, in their own feminine way. After all, sir, we are not at war now, and they do not know how to 'report' to a senior officer.'

Rhea watched him take a step back and gesture that she should step into his place to continue. Her father looked bemused but remained silent, which she took as her cue to begin. 'Thank you, Mr Williamson.' She smiled at him, then faced her father. 'We think Mrs Donaldson will live, but she had a difficult birth and is still very weak. The fever has gone, but only time will tell if she can come through this ordeal in good health.'

Rhea watched her father sit down while she had explained that Mrs Donaldson had been with child. It was as if his legs had given way under him as he sank into the chair. His faith in womanhood was being sorely tempted, she was certain. After all, who would have suspected that the timid Mrs Donaldson could have been living such a seemingly colourful double life?

'With child?' Francis repeated.

Rhea thought the shock must be overwhelming for him; but like the calm before the storm, she hoped he would not do anything that would threaten the wellbeing of either mother or baby. Mr Williamson stepped back further, calmly watching the scene unfold before him. To Rhea, her father's greying hair seemed to be turning more so since he returned home.

'You say she is weak, but well and … the baby also?' Francis asked.

'Dr Sanderson told us that she needs to stay here and be cared for, as she has lost much blood, Father,' Charlotte said. 'He promised he would keep the matter confidential and would speak to you, should you wish him to, once you were aware of the situation.'

'The baby is small, but seems strong, Father,' Rhea added.

'What do you girls know of such things? You should not be dealing with this,' Francis blurted out.

'It is life, Father, and we are women

now,' Charlotte said.

The major's tired eyes took in the image of both of his daughters and appeared to see them afresh. 'Yes, indeed,' he said, and looked at Travis. 'Yes, I see that you clearly are.'

17

'Take me to her,' the major commanded, and he stood up.

'Father, she is weak,' Charlotte said in alarm. 'Now may not be the time to — '

He rounded on her. 'You may not have a favourable impression of me, but please be assured I have never picked on a hapless woman in a time of great need.'

'I only meant — '

'Charlotte, I know what you meant, so do not try to humour me. Is she in her own room?'

'Yes, Father,' Charlotte replied.

'Good. Come with me. Rhea, you stay here and keep Mr Williamson company. I shall return shortly. Have Judd prepare the Oak Room.' He stormed out, with Charlotte following behind.

★ ★ ★

'Well,' Rhea said, 'that did not go well.'

'Believe me, Miss Rhea, that is not an angry man, but one who is coming to terms with a new situation. Your father's temper, when roused by his men, is a hundred times worse. He was worried for his daughters when he discovered that the matter at hand was an unusual one, and yet you have both coped well.' He stood next to her. 'You look tired and have not eaten. You should.'

'We asked Cook to prepare some cold food and leave it in the dining room under servers. I am sorry; we should have sent word to you. It was just that the baby needed … ' Her voice nearly broke. 'What must you think of us?' She looked into the deep brown pools of his eyes and knew that Charlotte had missed out on a golden opportunity to catch a good man; a handsome and considerate one. Going on an adventure with her father had seemed like a distant dream, just as Charlotte's of being a grand lady in a grand house had been.

'I told him what I think of you both,'

Travis said, 'and I meant it. I have nowhere else to be and nothing else to do, so I will help in any way I can.'

He was so close to Rhea that she could breathe in his musk. And she was so tired that if he put those strong arms around her, she would have happily sunk into their warmth. If she did, however, she suspected that her tiredness would dissipate and a new energy would be found, for whenever she was near this man she felt alive in a very new way.

'Thank you for being here.' The words slipped out of her mouth before she had even thought about what she should say.

'Rhea, this may not be the correct time, but may I ask you a direct question?'

'Mr Williamson, under the circumstances I think we can dispense with the normal formalities. Just ask what you will. If I can, I will answer honestly.'

He smiled down at her. 'It is this. If the major still would have me offer for his daughter's hand in marriage, could I ask that it would be acceptable to you if I tried to sway his thinking so that I may court you instead of your sister?'

She saw him swallow, and realised how disappointed he would be if she refused his request. Yet she was delighted that he had made the proposition. There was only one thing that made it unacceptable, however. 'But Charlotte is the elder daughter,' she told him, 'and should marry first.'

He sighed. 'Yes, but we know she clearly loves another. And even though my initial appraisal of her has been shown by this latest emergency to be incorrect, we could never be more than friends. But you ... ' He traced her cheek with his finger.

Rhea knew she should have stepped back, rebuked him or slapped his face, but she didn't. She wanted to tilt her head back and feel the taste and pressure of his lips on hers — and so much more.

He quickly kissed her lips, and then stepped back as if putting a deliberate distance between them. 'I apologise ... I should not have done that,' he said.

'I forgive you.' She smiled warmly, and

169

then remembered the woman in the bed and the baby at her side. Was that the cause of her fall? A single kiss awakening the desire for more — the warmth and touch of another human being who wanted her, but who had then deserted her? Rhea would not let Mr Williamson place her in that position, though she liked his proposition.

'If you can persuade my father,' she said, 'then I will happily be courted by you. I will speak to Charlotte of it. But you should know that my father has been planning to take me on a trip to the new world — to New South Wales — once you and Charlotte were wed. He knows you would be able to care for the estate, and he trusts you. But the truth is that I, too, know how to do so. I managed when he was at war. It was I who kept the place going, and I would hate to see it fall into evil days.' Rhea's passion rose along with her voice.

'You love the land. You love your home. Why would you want to travel to some under-developed place on the other side of the world?' Travis asked her.

'I always wanted to travel, and Father — '

'Rhea, think — what do you lack here that you think you can find in New South Wales? It is a penal colony; it is a harsh place.'

Rhea looked at Travis and realised that with him here — someone to help make the estate work, she did not think she would find what her heart truly desired in another land, near or far. 'But Father — '

'I will speak with him, if I have your blessing, and we shall see if this cannot work out best for all.'

★　★　★

Charlotte could hardly keep up with her father's pace as he hastened to Mrs Donaldson's room. Without waiting for her to enter first to make sure the woman was decent or presentable, he burst in. Charlotte's heart lifted when she saw Mrs Donaldson propped up on some pillows, with Cook at her side. The baby slept soundly in the cot.

'Mrs Donaldson, you look much rested,' Charlotte broke the awkward silence.

'Well I brushed her hair, and she looks so much like her old self,' Cook added awkwardly as the major stood there staring down at the baby. Then his eyes found Mrs Donaldson, and her own gaze met his without flinching. Charlotte admired her determination to stand her ground, even in such a poor situation; she had found her backbone as she had a baby — another life to fight for.

'Leave us.' Francis glanced at Cook. She scurried nervously away, patting Mrs Donaldson's arm as she did, as if wishing her good luck.

'Father … ' Charlotte began.

'You too,' he ordered.

'But I should stay.' He slowly turned his head to look down at her, and she could not help but recoil. 'Very well — but I will not be far away.' She stepped outside but deliberately left the door slightly ajar. Then she told Cook to make some soup to go with the cold fare so that her father might eat something warm after his journey. However, she really wanted the servant away from the corridor so she could put her ear to the crack and listen in.

'Dorothea, you never said anything to me about being with child. Why?'

Charlotte watched as Francis moved nearer to Mrs Donaldson. Dorothea … Charlotte had not known what her Christian name was.

'I didn't realise for quite a time,' Mrs Donaldson answered. 'I have never been of a big frame. I had thought myself unable to bear one. I presumed the fault had lain within me and not my husband, but it appears that I was wrong. So his mother need not have resented me to her grave, after all.'

'Did you think I would turn you out?' Francis asked, his voice gentle. 'Did you think so little of me that you believed I would do anything less than the honourable thing?'

Charlotte was beginning to feel uneasy.

Why was he not demanding to know who the father was? She knew her father had known Mrs Donaldson's husband, and possibly felt some duty of care toward her, but there was more to this than met the eye. Was he actually saying that he …

'It is a boy,' Mrs Donaldson's soft voice informed him.

'A boy!' The major's voice almost cracked with emotion.

Charlotte heard movement and guessed her father was moving over to the baby to take a look at him.

'He is small, but he is strong, Francis.'

Francis! Charlotte's stomach began to flutter as realisation dawned upon her. One that she hoped beyond hope was true.

'He is a fine, son.' The major's voice, now stronger, was undeniably filled with pride.

Charlotte put a hand over her mouth. There was no doubt: her father had sired a son and heir, if he did do the honourable thing and acknowledge it.

This would mean that Charlotte did

not have to marry Mr Williamson. She would be free of the duty to provide the next heir, in order to make up for her father's inability to do so. He had managed it after all. Charlotte bit her knuckle to stop a gasp escaping. She should be appalled, but she was not.

'You will grow strong, Dorothea, you and the child, and then you will accompany me on a journey I have to take to fulfil a business arrangement. It will mean that Rhea will now need to stay, as I have the tickets and all is planned. She will be disappointed; but you have four months to recover, and then you will travel as Mrs Buckleby — and when we return, we may have more children.'

Charlotte heard the woman laugh. 'Yes, I will be Mrs Buckleby, if that is what you are proposing, Francis. But I am weak and have nearly died. I will not risk my life or that of our son on one of your ventures. You go if you must; I will be here when you return.'

'I have obligations!' he said, but his voice was not harsh.

'Then send someone in your stead.'

Charlotte heard her father gasp. 'Send me,' she said as she burst into the room.

Her father turned to look at her, seemingly unsurprised to discover that she had been eavesdropping. 'Don't be ridiculous,' he said. 'What would you know? You are to marry Travis,' he said.

'No, Father — but Rhea may very well do so. Send me with a man who is hardy and whom you trust ... Jenkins.' Charlotte saw Mrs Donaldson smile at the major's flustered face.

Rhea appeared in the doorway with Travis behind her. Charlotte pointed to the baby. 'Meet your half-brother, Rhea,' she said with a smile.

'Father!' Rhea exclaimed. 'You have had an affair behind our backs, in our own home, and you preach to us about being proper.'

He ignored Rhea's comment and the stunned expression upon her face. 'Why would you want to go to New South Wales with Jenkins?' he asked Charlotte. 'It is hardly appropriate.'

'Appropriate? Yet it is fine for you to seduce the housekeeper!' Charlotte snapped.

Travis put a comforting and protective hand on Rhea's shoulder. She did not pull away from it.

The major looked at his daughters. 'I did not seduce Dorothea in the way you mean. She and I fell in love. Are you telling me,' he continued, addressing Charlotte, 'that with all your fancy dreams and aspirations, you have fallen for my man Jenkins?'

'Yes, I have.' She smiled at her father as he shook his head.

'Your mother would blame me for this, and I cannot deny it is all of my making. If I send Jenkins on this trip, then you will go with him as his wife. The colonies welcome new blood and money. But once you have chosen your path, Charlotte, you have to make it work. You cannot turn back. He is a good man, the salt of the earth. Treat him kindly.' He did not smile at the last comment, but both Rhea and Charlotte gasped as they realised he actually meant what he had said.

'That leaves you, Travis,' Francis said, turning to Mm. 'It seems I have brought you here to be usurped by your sergeant.'

Rhea reached up and placed her hand over Travis' fingers. 'It does not matter, Father; for while your heir is growing stronger, we can help make the estate work to provide a good living for us all. If a union between Travis and myself meets with your approval, we would like to spend that time getting to know and understand each other better. Travis may still repay his debt to you, but with a willing heart this time.' She smiled at Charlotte, who nodded.

Francis gave a long sigh as he gazed at his daughters. 'Very well, Charlotte — this time I will grant you your wish. I have my heart's desire; and after I have recovered from affording Charlotte's wedding and all her new attire, I shall marry Dorothea.' Then he looked at Travis. 'If all is well between you and Rhea, I would happily welcome you into my family, Travis, as my son. I have never had one before now, and you have been as one to me through the bloodshed of war. I would have that relationship with you in peacetime too.'

Rhea turned to see how Travis's eyes welled up as he fought to hold back a flood of emotion. 'Thank you,' he managed to say. 'I'd be honoured.'

The major stood. 'Good; that's sorted, then. You get strong.' He kissed Dorothea on her forehead somewhat self-consciously, then glanced at the sleeping baby. 'You too.' Turning to Charlotte, he said, 'You be strong,' and to Rhea and Travis, 'You find the strength of love within each other — for there is nothing more powerful on this earth than the love that binds people together.'

HEART OF THE MOUNTAIN

Carol MacLean

Emotionally burned out from her job as a nurse, Beth leaves London for the Scottish Highlands and the peace of her aunt's cottage. Here she meets Alex, a man who is determined to live life to the full after the death of his fiancée in a climbing accident. Despite her wish for a quiet life, Beth is pulled into a friendship with Alex's sister, bubbly Sarah-Jayne, and finds herself increasingly drawn to Alex . . .

MIDSUMMER MAGIC

Julie Coffin

Fearing that her ex-husband plans to take their daughter away with him to New Zealand, Lauren escapes with little Amy to the remote Cornish cottage bequeathed to her by her Great-aunt Hilda. But Lauren had not even been aware of Hilda's existence until now, so why was the house left to her and not local schoolteacher Adam Poldean, who seemed to be Hilda's only friend? Lauren sets out to learn the answers — and finds herself becoming attracted to the handsome Adam as well.

DANGEROUS WATERS

Sheila Daglish

On holiday in the enchanting Hungarian village of Szentendre, schoolteacher Cassandra Sutherland meets handsome local artist Matthias Benedek, and soon both are swept up in a romance as dreamy as the moon on the Danube. But Matt is hiding secrets from Cass, and she is determined never to love another man like her late fiancé, whose knack for getting into dangerous situations was the ruin of them both. Can love conquer all once it's time for Cass to return home to London?

THE MAGIC OF THORN HOUSE

Christina Green

After the death of her dear Aunt Jem, Carla Marshall inherits Thorn House, the ancient country manor where she spent a happy childhood. But her arrival brings with it fresh problems. She meets and falls in love with local bookseller Dan Eastern — but is he only after the long-lost manuscript of one of Aunt Jem's books, which would net him a fortune if Carla can find it? And her aunt's Memory Box hides a secret that's about to turn Carla's world upside down . . .